"Every morning Tiger and Tom stood faithfully in the market-place."
(See page 12.)

Tiger and Tom

and

Other Stories for Boys

"Words Fitly Spoken"
Every Story Contains an Important Lesson

SABBATH READINGS

FOR THE HOME CIRCLE

AUTHORIZED   EDITION

SOUTHERN PUBLISHING ASSOCIATION

Nashville, Tennessee

Fort Worth, Texas   Atlanta, Georgia

The stories in this book were complied from a four volume set titled, Sabbath Readings. The stories were orginally gathered from church papers in the 1870's, Methodists, Lutheran, Presbyterian, etc. We bring to you this 1910 reproduction, which is when the stories were first illustrated. We have found the stories to be truly "a breath of fresh air" in literature for children and youth. May they receive a warm welcome in your home is our prayer.

The Publishers.

Republished by:
A B Publishing
(Angela's Bookshelf)
9746 N. Mason Road
Wheeler, Mi 48662
Cover Artist:
James Converse
COPYRIGHTED 1993 by:
A B Publishing

CONTENTS

ILLUSTRATIONS

TIGER AND TOM

THE day was pleasant, in that particularly pleasant part of summer time, which the boys call "vacation," when Tiger and Tom walked slowly down the street together.

You may think it strange that I mention Tiger first, but I assure you, Tom would not have been in the least offended by the preference. Indeed, he would have told you that Tiger was a most wonderful dog, and knew as much as any two boys, though this might be called extravagant.

Nearly a year ago, on Tom's birthday, Tiger arrived as a present from Tom's uncle, and as the dog leaped with a dignified bound from the wagon in which he made his journey, Tom looked for a moment into his great, wise eyes, and impulsively threw his arms around his shaggy neck.

Tiger was pleased with Tom's bright face, and affectionately licked his smooth cheeks. So the league of friendship was complete in an hour.

Tom had a pleasant, round face, and you might

live with him a week, and think him one of the
noblest, most generous boys you ever knew. But
some day you would probably discover that he
had a most violent temper.

You would be frightened to see his face crimson
with rage, as he stamped his feet, shook his little
sister, spoke improperly to his mother, and above
all, displeased his
great Father in
heaven.

Now I am going to
tell you of something
which happened to
Tom, on this ac-
count, which he
never forgot to the
end of his life.

Tiger and Tom
were walking down
the street together
one pleasant day,
when they met Dick
Casey, a schoolfellow of Tom's.

"O Dick!" cried Tom, "I'm going to father's
grain store a little while. Let's go up in the
loft and play."

Dick had just finished his work in his mother's
garden, and was ready for a little amusement.
So the two went up in the loft together, and
enjoyed themselves for a long time.

But at last one of those trifling disputes arose,

in which little boys are so apt to indulge. Pretty
soon there were angry words, then (Oh, how sorry
I am to say it!) Tom's wicked passions got the
mastery of him, and he beat little Dick severely.

Tiger, who must have been ashamed of his master, pulled hard at his coat, and whined piteously,
but all in vain. At last Tom stopped, from mere
exhaustion.

"There, now!" he
cried, "which is right,
you or I?"

"I am," sobbed
Dick, "and you tell a
lie."

Tom's face became
crimson, and darting
upon Dick, he gave
him a sudden push.
Alas! he was near to
the open door. Dick
screamed, threw up
his arms, and in a
moment was gone.

Tom's heart stood still, and an icy chill crept
over him from head to foot. At first he could
not stir; then—he never knew how he got there,
but he found himself standing beside his little
friend. Some men were raising him carefully
from the hard sidewalk.

"Is he dead?" almost screamed Tom.

"No," replied one, "we hope not. How did he
fall out?"

"He did'nt fall," groaned Tom, who never could be so mean as to tell a lie, "I pushed him out."

"*You* pushed him, you wicked boy," cried a rough voice. "Do you know you ought to be sent to jail, and if he dies, maybe you'll be hung."

Tom grew as white as Dick, whom he had followed into the store, and he heard all that passed as if in a dream.

"Is he badly hurt?" cried some one.

"Only his hands," was the answer. "The rope saved him, he caught hold of the rope and slipped down; but his hands are dreadfully torn—he has fainted from pain.

Just then Tom's father came in, and soon understood the case. The look he gave his unhappy son, so full of sorrow, not unmingled with pity, was too much for Tom, and he stole out followed by the faithful Tiger.

He wandered to the woods, and threw himself upon the ground. One hour ago he was a happy boy, and now what a terrible change! What had made the difference?—Nothing but the indulgence of this wicked, violent temper.

His mother had often warned him of the fearful consequences. She had told him that little boys who would not learn to govern themselves, grew up to be very wicked men, and often became murderers in some moment of passion.

And now, Tom shuddered to think he was almost a murderer! Nothing but God's great mercy in putting that rope in Dick's way, had saved him from carrying that load of sorrow and guilt all the rest of his life.

But poor Dick might die yet—how pale he looked—how strange! Tom fell upon his knees, and prayed God to spare Dick's life, and from that time forth, with God's help, he promised that he would strive to conquer his wicked temper.

Then, as he could no longer bear his terrible suspense, he started for Widow Casey's cottage. As he appeared at the humble door, Mrs. Casey angrily ordered him away, saying, "You have made a poor woman trouble enough for one day." But Dick's feeble voice entreated, "O mother, let him come in ; I was just as bad as he."

Tom gave a cry of joy at hearing these welcome tones, and sprang hastily in. There sat poor Dick, with his hands bound up, looking very pale, but Tom thanked God that he was alive.

"I should like to know how I am to live now," sighed Mrs. Casey. "Who will weed the garden, and carry my vegetables to market? I am afraid we shall suffer for bread before the summer is over," and she put her apron to her eyes.

"Mrs. Casey," cried Tom, eagerly, "I will do everything that Dick did. I will sell the cabbages, potatoes, and beans, and will drive Mr. Brown's cows to pasture."

Mrs. Casey shook her head incredulously ; but Tom bravely kept his word. For the next few weeks Tom was at his post bright and early, and the garden was never kept in better order.

Every morning Tiger and Tom stood faithfully
in the market place with their baskets, and never
gave up, no matter how warm the day, till the last
vegetable was sold, and the money placed faithfully
in Mrs. Casey's hand.

Tom's father often passed through the market,
and gave his little son an encouraging smile, but
he did not offer to help him out of his difficulty,
for he knew if Tom struggled on alone, it would
be a lesson he would never forget. Already he was
becoming so gentle and patient that every one
noticed the change, and his mother rejoiced over
the sweet fruits of his repentance and self-sacrifice.

After a few weeks, the bandages were removed
from Dick's hands, but they had been unskillfully
treated, and were drawn up in very strange shapes.

Mrs. Casey could not conceal her grief. "He
will never be the help he was before," she said to
Tom, "he will never be like other boys, and he
wrote such a fine hand; now he can no more make
a letter than that little chicken in the garden."

"If we only had a great city doctor," said a neighbor, "he might have been all right. Even now his
fingers might be helped if you should take him to
New York."

"Oh, I am too poor, *too poor*," said she, and burst
into tears.

Tom could not bear it, and again rushed into the
woods to think what could be done, for he had already given them all his quarter's allowance. All
at once a thought flashed into his head, and he

started as if he had been shot. Then he cried in great distress:—

"No, no, anything but that, I can't do *that!*"

Tiger gently licked his hands, and watched him with great concern.

Now came a terrible struggle. Tom paced back and forth, and although he was a proud boy, he sobbed aloud. Tiger whined, licked Tom's face, rushed off into dark corners, and barked savagely at some imagi-
nary enemy, and then came back, and putting his paws on his young master's knees, wagged his tail in anxious sym-
pathy.

At last Tom took his hands from his pale, tear stained face, and looking into the dog's great, honest eyes, he cried with a queer shake in his voice:—

"Tiger, old fellow! dear old dog, could you ever forgive me if I sold you?"

Then came another burst of sorrow, and Tom rose hastily, as if afraid to trust himself, and almost ran out of the woods. Over the fields he raced, with Tiger close at his heels, nor rested a moment till he stood at Major White's door, nearly two miles away.

"Do you still want Tiger, sir?"

"Why yes," said the old man in great surprise, "but it can't be possible that you want to sell him, do you, my boy?" and the kind old gentleman gave Tom a quick, questioning glance.

"Yes, please," gasped Tom, not daring to look at his old companion.

The exchange was quickly made, and the ten dollars in Tom's hand. Tiger was beguiled into a barn, the door hastily shut, and Tom was hurrying off, when he turned and cried in a choking voice:—

"You will be kind to him, Major White, won't you? Don't whip him, I never did, and he's the best dog—"

"No, no, child," said Major White, kindly; "I'll treat him like a prince, and if you ever want to buy him back, you shall have him."

Tom managed to falter "Thank you," and almost flew out of hearing of Tiger's eager scratching on the barn door.

I am making my story too long, and can only tell you in a few words that Tom's sacrifice was accepted. A friend took little Dick to the city free of expense, and Tom's money paid for the necessary operation.

The poor, crooked fingers were very much improved, and were soon almost as good as ever. And the whole village loved Tom for his brave, self-sacrificing spirit, and the noble atonement he had made for his moment of passion.

A few days after Dick's return came Tom's birth-

day, but he did not feel in his usual spirits. In
spite of his delight in Dick's recovery, he had so
mourned over the matter, and had taken Tiger's
loss so much to heart, that he had grown quite
pale and thin. So as he was allowed to spend the
day as he pleased, he took his books and went to
his favorite haunt in the woods. He lay down
under the shade of a wide-spreading maple, and
buried his face in his hands : —

"How different from my last birthday," thought
Tom. "Then Tiger had just come, and I was so
happy, though I didn't like him half as well as I
do now."

Tom sighed heavily; then added more cheerfully,
"Well, I hope some things are better than they
were last year. I hope I have begun to conquer
myself, and with God's help I will never give up
trying while I live. But O how much sorrow and
misery I have made for myself as well as for others,
by only once giving way to my wicked, foolish
temper. And not only that, but," added Tom,
with a sigh, "I can never forget that I might
have been a murderer, had it not been for the
mercy of God. Now if I could only earn money
enough to buy back dear old Tiger."

While Tom was busied with these thoughts, he
heard a hasty, familiar trot, a quick bark of joy,
and the brave old dog sprang into Tom's arms.

"Tiger, old fellow," cried Tom, trying to look
fierce, though he could scarcely keep down the
tears, "how came you to run away, sir?"

Tiger responded by picking up a letter he had dropped in his first joy, and laying it in Tom's hand:—

"MY DEAR CHILD: Tiger is pining, and I must give him a change of air. I wish him to have a good master, and knowing that the best ones are those who have learned to govern *themselves*, I send him to you. Will you take care of him and oblige

Your old friend,   MAJOR WHITE."

Tom then read through a mist of tears—:

"P. S. I know the whole story. Dear young friend, be not weary in well doing.'"

"THOSE SCARS"

W HAT are those scars?" questioned Mary Lan-
man of her father as she sat in his lap, holding
his hand in her own little ones.

"Those scars, my dear? If I were to tell you
the history of them, it would make a long story."

"But do tell me, papa," said Mary, "I should
like to hear a long story."

"These scars, my child, are more than forty
years old. For forty years they have every day reminded me of my disobedience to my parents and
my violation of the law of God."

"Do tell me all about it, father," pleaded Mary.

"When I was about twelve years old," he began,
"my father sent me one pleasant autumn day into
the woods to cut a pole to be used in beating apples
off the trees. It was wanted immediately to fill
the place of one that had been broken.

I took my little hatchet and hastened to the
woods as I had been bidden. I looked in every
direction for a tall, slender tree that would answer

the purpose ; and every time I stopped to examine a young tree, a taller and straighter sapling caught my eye farther on.

"What seemed most surprising to me was that the little trees that looked so trim and upright in the distance, grew deformed and crooked as I approached them. Frequently disappointed, I was led from tree to tree, till I had traversed the entire grove and made no choice.

"My path opened into a clearing, and near the fence stood a young cherry tree loaded with fruit. Here was a strong temptation. I knew very well to whom this tree belonged, and that it bore valuable fruit. I knew, too, that I had no right to touch a single cherry. No house was near, no person was in sight. None but God could see me, and I forgot that His eye looked down upon me.

"I resolved to taste the tempting fruit. I climbed the tree and began to pick the rich, ripe cherries. But I found no pleasure in the taste of them; I was so fearful of surprise and detection. Some one might come and find me in the tree. I therefore resolved to break off some richly-loaded boughs, and feast upon the cherries as I hastened home.

"The top of the tree was bowed with the weight of its fruit. I climbed as high as I could, and bending down the top, attempted to cut it off with my knife. In my eagerness to secure my prize, I did not guard my left hand, which held down the top of the tree. My knife slipped from the yielding wood to my fingers, and passed with unspent force across all the fingers of my left hand, cutting the flesh to the bone.

"I never could look at fresh blood without fainting. My eye caught sight of the red drops that oozed from every finger, and my heart began to die within me. I slipped through the limbs of the tree to the ground. The shock of the fall drove away the faintness, and I soon stood upon my feet.

"I wrapped my handkerchief about my bleeding fingers, and hurried home. My mission was worse than useless; I had not accomplished the purpose for which I was sent, I had committed a crime and disabled myself for work ; for how could I pick apples in my present condition.

"I found no sympathy from anybody ; my father reproved me, and threatened chastisement whe" my wounds were healed. My mother, who dressed my aching fingers, looked very sorrowfully upon me, and I knew that I had grieved her deeply by my disobedience.

"I assisted in picking the apples, but I was compelled to work with one hand, while the other hung in a sling. That was a sad day for me.

"It required some weeks to heal the deep gashes made by my knife, and the scars are as bright, after forty years, as they were when the wounds were first closed.

"But if the scars in the flesh were all, it would have been comparatively a trifle. But the soul was wounded as well as the body. The conscience was defiled with guilt. Tears of repentance could not wipe away the stain. Nothing but the blood of Christ could give health to the wounded spirit.

"As wounds leave scars, so, my dear child, youthful sins leave the traces of their existence. Like the scars of the healed wound, they disfigure and weaken the soul. The follies of youth may be overcome, but they are always sure to leave their mark. Every sin of childhood hangs like a weight upon the neck of manhood. The blood of Jesus Christ alone cleanseth from all sin."

COALS OF FIRE

GUY MORGAN came in from school with rapid step and impetuous manner. His mother looked up from her work. There was a round, red spot on his cheek, and an ominous glitter in his eyes. She knew the signs. His naturally fierce temper had been stirred in some way to a heat that had kindled his whole nature. He tossed down his cap, threw himself on an ottoman at her feet, and then said, with still a little of the heat of his temper in his tone, "Never say, after this, that I don't love you, mother."

"I think I never did say so," she answered gently, as she passed her hand over the tawny locks, and brushed them away from the flushed brow. "But what special thing have you done to prove your love for me just now?"

"Taken a blow without returning it."

She bent over and kissed her boy. He was fifteen years old, a tall fellow with strong muscles; but he had not grown above liking his mother's kisses.

Then she said softly, "Tell me all about it, Guy."

"O, it was Dick Osgood! You know what a mean fellow he is, anyhow. He had been tormenting some of the younger boys till I could not stand it. Every one of them is afraid of him.

"I told him he ought to be ashamed of himself,

and tried to make him leave off, till, after a while, he turned from them, and coming to me, he struck me in the face. I believe the mark is there now;" and he turned the other cheek toward his mother. Her heart was filled with sympathy and secret indignation.

"Well," she said, "and you—what did you do?"

"I remembered what I had promised you for this year, and I took it—think of it, mother—took it, and never touched him! I just looked into his eyes, and said, 'If I should strike you back, I should lower myself to your level.'

"He laughed a great, scornful laugh, and said, 'You hear, boys, Morgan's turned preacher. You'd better wait, sir, before you lecture me on my behavior to the little ones, till you have pluck enough to defend them. I've heard about the last impudence I shall from a coward like you.'

"The boys laughed, and some of them said, 'Good for you, Osgood!' and I came home. I had done it for the sake of my promise to you! for I'm stronger than he is, any day; and *you* know, mother, whether there's a drop of coward's blood in my veins. I thought you were the one to comfort me; though it is n't comfort I want so much, either. I just want you to release me from that promise, and let me go back and thrash him."

Mrs. Morgan's heart thrilled with silent thanksgiving. Her boy's temper had been her greatest grief. His father was dead, and she had brought him up alone, and sometimes she was afraid her too great tenderness had spoiled him.

She had tried in vain to curb his passionate nature. It was a power which no bands could bind. She had concluded at last that the only hope was in enlisting his own powerful will, and making him resolve to conquer himself. Now he had shown himself capable of self-control. In the midst of his anger he had remembered his pledge to her, and had kept it. He would yet be his own master,—this brave boy of hers,—and the kingdom of his own mind would be a goodly sovereignty.

"Better heap coals of fire on his head!" she said quietly.

"Yes, he deserves a good scorching,"—pretending to misunderstand her,—"but I should not have thought *you* would be so revengeful."

"You know well enough what kind of coals I mean, and *who* it was that said, 'If thine enemy hunger, feed him ; if he thirst, give him drink.' I can not release you from your promise till the year for which you made it is over.

"I think that the Master who told us to render good for evil, understood all the wants and passions of humanity better than any other teacher has ever understood them. I am sure that what He said must be wise and right and best. I want you to try His way first. If that fails, there will be time enough after this year to make a different experiment."

"Well, I promised you," he said, "and I'll show you that, at least, I'm strong enough to keep my word until you release me from it. I think, though, you do n't quite know how hard it is."

Mrs. Morgan knew that it was very hard for a true, brave-hearted boy to be called a coward; but she knew, also, that the truest bravery on earth is the bravery of endurance.

"Look out for the coals of fire!" she said smilingly, as her boy started for school the next morning. "Keep a good watch, and I'm pretty sure you'll find them before the summer is over."

But he came home at night depressed and a little gloomy. There had always been a sort of rivalry between him and Dick Osgood, and now the boys seemed to have gone over to the stronger side, and he had that bitter feeling of humiliation and disgrace, which is as bitter to a boy as the sense of defeat ever is to a man.

The weeks went on, and the feeling wore away

a little. Still the memory of that blow rankled in Guy's mind, and made him unsocial and ill at ease. His mother watched him with some anxiety, but did not interfere. She had the true wisdom to leave him to learn some of the lessons of life alone.

At length came the last day of school, followed next day by a picnic, in which all the scholars, superintended by their teachers, were to join.

Guy Morgan hesitated a little and then concluded to go. The place selected was a lovely spot, known in all the neighborhood as "the old mill." It was on the banks of the Quassit River, where the stream ran fast, and the grass was green, and great trees with drooping boughs shut away the July sunlight.

Among the rest were Dick Osgood and his little sister Hetty, the one human being whom he seemed really and tenderly to love. The teacher's eyes were on him for this one day, and he did not venture to insult the older scholars or domineer over the little ones. He and Guy kept apart as much as they conveniently could; and Guy entered into the spirit of the day, and really enjoyed it much better than he had anticipated.

Dinner was spread on the grass, and though it was eaten with pewter spoons, and out of crockery of every hue and kind, it was certainly eaten with greater enjoyment and keener appetite than if it had been served in the finest dining room.

They made dinner last as long as they could, and then they scattered here and there, to enjoy themselves as they liked.

"Guy Morgan caught her by her long, golden hair."

On the bridge, just above the falls, stood a little group, fishing. Among them were Dick Osgood and his sister. Guy Morgan, always deeply interested in the study of botany, was a little distance away, with one of the teachers, pulling in pieces a curious flower.

Suddenly a wild cry arose above the sultry stillness of the summer afternoon and the hum of quiet voices round. It was Dick Osgood's cry: "She's in, boys! Hetty's in the river, and *I* can't swim. O, save her! save her! Will *no* one try?"

Before the words were out of his lips, they all saw Guy Morgan coming with flying feet,—a race for life. He unbuttoned coat and vest as he ran, and cast them off as he neared the bridge. He kicked off his shoes, and threw himself over.

They heard him strike the water. He went under, rose again, and then struck out toward the golden head, which just then rose for the second time. Every one who stood there lived moments which seemed hours.

Mr. Sharp, the teacher with whom Guy had been talking, and some of the boys, got a strong rope, and running down the stream, threw it out on the water just above the falls, where Guy could reach it if he could get so near the shore—*if!*

The water was very deep where Hetty had fallen in, and the river ran fast. It was sweeping the poor child on, and Dick Osgood threw himself upon the bridge, and sobbed and screamed. When she rose the third time, she was near the falls. A moment more and she would go over, down on the jagged, cruel rocks beneath.

But that time Guy Morgan caught her—caught her by her long, glistening, golden hair. Mr. Sharp shouted to him. He saw the rope, and swam toward it, his strong right arm beating the water back with hammer-strokes—his left motionless, holding his white burden.

"O God!" Mr. Sharp prayed fervently, "keep him up, spare his strength a little longer, a little longer!" A moment more and he reached the rope and clung to it desperately, while teacher and boys drew the two in over the slippery edge, out of the horrible, seething waters, and took them in their arms. But they were both silent and motionless. Mr. Sharp spoke Guy's name, but he did not answer. Would either of them ever answer again?

Teachers and scholars went to work alike for their restoration. It was well that there was intelligent guidance, or their best efforts might have failed.

Guy, being the stronger, was first to revive. "Is Hetty safe?" he asked.

"Only God knows?" Mr. Sharp answered. "We are doing our best."

It was almost half an hour before Hetty opened her blue eyes. Meantime Dick had been utterly frantic and helpless. He had sobbed and groaned and even prayed, in a wild fashion of his own, which perhaps the pitying Father understood and answered.

When he heard his sister's voice, he was like one

beside himself with joy; but Mr. Sharp quieted
him by a few low, firm words, which no one else
understood.

Some of the larger girls arranged one of the
wagons, and received Hetty into it.

Mr. Sharp drove home with Guy Morgan. When
he reached his mother's gate, Guy insisted on going
in alone. He thought it might alarm her to see
some one helping him; besides, he wanted her a
few minutes quite·to himself. So Mr. Sharp drove
away, and Guy went in. His mother saw him
coming, and opened the door.

"Where have you been?" she cried, seeing his
wet, disordered plight.

"In Quassit River, mother, fishing out Hetty
Osgood."

Then, while she was busying herself with prepa-
rations for his comfort, he quietly told his story.
His mother's eyes were dim, and her heart throbbed
chokingly.

"O, if *you* had been drowned, my boy, my dar-
ling!" she cried, hugging him close, wet as he
was. "If I had been there, Guy, I couldn't have
let you do it."

"I went in after the coals of fire, mother."

Mrs. Morgan knew how to laugh as well as to
cry over her boy. "I've heard of people smart
enough to set the river on fire," she said, "but you
are the first one I ever knew who went in there
after the coals."

The next morning came a delegation of the

boys, with Dick Osgood at their head. Every one was there who had seen the blow which Dick struck, and heard his taunts afterward. They came into the sitting room, and said their say to Guy before his mother. Dick was spokesman.

"I have come," he said, "to ask you to forgive me. I struck you a mean, unjustifiable blow. You received it with noble contempt. To provoke you into fighting, I called you a coward, meaning to bring you down by some means to my own level. You bore that, too, with a greatness I was not great enough to understand; but I do understand it now.

"I have seen you—all we boys have seen you— face to face with Death, and have seen that you were not afraid of him. You fought with him, and came off ahead; and we all are come to do honor to the bravest boy in town; and I to thank you for a life a great deal dearer and better worth saving than my own."

Dick broke down just there, for the tears choked him.

Guy was as grand in his forgiveness as he had been in his forbearance.

Hetty and her father and mother came afterward, and Guy found himself a hero before he knew it. But none of it all moved him as did his mother's few fond words, and the pride in her joyful eyes. He had kept, with honor and with peace, his pledge to her, and he had his reward. The Master's way of peace had not missed him.

LYMAN DEAN'S TESTIMONIALS

I DO not believe two more excellent people could be found than Gideon Randal and his wife. To lift the fallen and to minister to the destitute was their constant habit and delight. They often sacrificed their own comforts for the benefit of others. In vain their friends protested at this course; Gideon Randal's unfailing reply was:—

"I think there's enough left to carry Martha and me through life, and some besides. What we give to the poor, we lend to the Lord, and if a dark day comes, He will provide."

The "dark day" came; but it was not until he had reached the age of three score and ten years. As old age came upon him, and his little farm became less productive, debts accumulated. Being forced to raise money, he had borrowed a thousand dollars of Esquire Harrington, giving him a mortgage on his home for security. But as the interest was regularly paid, his creditor was well satisfied. However, Mr. Harrington died suddenly, and his son, a merciless, grasping man, wrote Mr. Randal, demanding payment of the mortgage.

Vainly did the old man plead for an extension of time. The demand was pressed to such an extent that it even become a threat to deprive him of his home unless payment were made within a given time.

"Martha," he said to his wife, "young Harrington is a hard man. He has me in his power, and he will not scruple to ruin me. I think I would better go and talk with him, telling him how little I have. It may be he will pity two old people, and allow us better terms."

"But husband, you are not used to traveling; Harrowtown is a hundred miles away, and you are old and feeble too."

"True, wife; but I can talk much better than I can write, and besides, Luke Conway lives there, you remember. I took an interest in him when he was a poor boy; perhaps he will advise and help us, now that we are in trouble."

At last, since he felt that he must go, Mrs. Randal reluctantly consented, and fitted him out for the journey with great care.

The next morning was warm and sunny for November, and the old man started for Harrowtown.

"Gideon," called Mrs. Randal as he walked slowly down the road, "be sure to take tight hold of the railing, when you get in and out of the cars."

"I'll be careful, Martha," and with one more

"good bye" wave of his hand, the old man hurried on to take the stage, which was to carry him to the station. But misfortune met him at the very outset. The stage was heavily loaded, and on the way, one of the wheels broke down; this caused such a delay that Mr. Randal missed the morning train, and the next did not come for several hours.

It was afternoon when he finally started. He became anxious and weary from long waiting, and after three stations were passed, he became nervous and worried.

"How long before we reach Harrowtown?" he inquired, stopping the busy conductor.

"At half past eight."

Another question was upon Mr. Randal's lips, but the conductor was gone. "Not reach there until evening!"

"How long before we reach Harrowtown?"

he exclaimed to himself in dismay, "and pitch dark, for there's no moon now; I shall not know where to go!"

Presently the conductor passed again. "Mr. Conductor, will you kindly tell me when to get out?

I've never been to Harrowtown, and I do n't want to stop at the wrong place."

"Give yourself no uneasiness," was the polite reply, "I'll let you know; I will not forget you."

Soothed by this assurance, the old man settled back in his seat and finally went to sleep.

In the seat behind him sat a tall, handsome boy. His name was Albert Gregory. He was bright and intelligent, but there was an expression of cruelty about his mouth, and a look about his eyes that was cold and unfeeling. This lad saw the old man fall asleep, and he nudged his companion :—

"See here, John, by and by I'll play a good joke on that old country greeny, and you 'll see fun."

On rushed the train; mile after mile was passed. Daylight faded, and the lamps were lighted in the cars, and still the old man slept, watched by his purposed tormentor and the other boy, who wanted to see "the fun."

At last the speed of the train began to slacken. They were nearing a station. Albert sprang up and shook Mr. Randal violently.

"Wake up! wake up!" he called sharply. "This is Harrowtown. You must get off here!"

Thus roughly roused, the old man started from his seat and gazed around in a bewildered way. The change from daylight to darkness, the unaccustomed awakening on a moving train, and the glare of the lights added tenfold to his confusion.

"Wh— what did you say, boy?" he asked helplessly.

"This is Harrowtown. The place where you want to stop. You must get off. Be quick, or you 'll be carried by."

The noise of the brakes, and ignorance of the real locality on the part of those near enough to have heard him, prevented any correction of the boy's cruel falsehood.

Mr. Randal knew it was not the conductor who had aroused him; but, supposing Albert to be some employee of the road, he hurried to the car door with tottering steps. The name of the station was called at the other end of the car,—a name

"This is Harrowtown. Be quick, or you 'll be carried by."

quite unlike that of "Harrowtown," but his dull ears did not notice it. He got off upon the platform, and before he could recover himself or knew his error, the train was again in motion.

Albert was in ecstasies over the success of his "joke," and shook all over with laughter, in which, of course, his companion joined. "O dear! that's jolly fun!" he cried, "is n't it, John?"

John assented that it was very funny indeed.

Neither of the boys had noticed that the seat lately occupied by the poor old man had just been taken by a fine-looking gentleman, wrapped in a heavy cloak, who appeared to be absorbed in his own thoughts, but who really heard every word they said.

They kept up a brisk conversation, Albert speaking in a loud tone, for he was feeling very merry. "Ha, ha, ha!—but I did think the old fool would hear the brakeman call the station, though. I didn't suppose I could get him any farther than the door. To think of his clambering clear out on the platform, and getting left! He believed every word I told him. What a delicious old simpleton!"

And having exhausted that edifying subject for the moment, he presently began to boast of his plans and prospects.

"I don't believe you stand much of a chance there; they say Luke Conway's awful particular," the stranger heard John remark.

"Pooh! shut up!" cried Albert. "Particular! That's just it, and that makes my chance all the better. I've brought the kind of recommendations that a particular man wants, you see."

"But there'll be lots of other fellows trying for the place."

"Don't care if there's fifty," said Albert, "I'd come in ahead of 'em all. I've got testimonials of character and qualifications from Prof. Howe, Rev. Joseph Lee, Dr. Henshaw, and Esq. Jenks, the great railroad contractor. His name alone is enough to secure me the situation."

At this, the gentleman on the next seat turned and gave Albert a quick, searching glance. But the conceited boy was too much occupied with himself to notice the movement, and kept on talking. Now and then the thought of the victim whom he had so cruelly deceived seemed to come back and amuse him amazingly.

"Wonder where the old man is now. Ha, ha! Do you suppose he has found out where Harrowtown is? Oh, but was n't it rich to see how scared he was when I awoke him? And how he jumped and scrambled out of the car! 'Pon my word, I never saw anything so comical."

Here the stranger turned again and shot another quick glance, this time from indignant eyes, and his lips parted as if about to utter a stern reproof. But he did not speak.

We will now leave Albert and his fellow-travelers, and follow good Gideon Randal.

It was quite dark when he stepped from the cars. "Can you tell me where I can find Mr. Aaron Harrington?" he inquired of a man at the station.

"There's no such man living here, to my knowledge," was the reply.

"What, is n't this Harrowtown?" asked Mr. Randal, in great consternation.

"No, it is Whipple Village."

"Then I got out at the wrong station. What shall I do?" in a voice of deep distress.

"Go right to the hotel and stay till the train goes in the morning," said the man, pleasantly.

There was no alternative. Mr. Randal passed a restless night at the hotel, and at an early hour he was again at the station, waiting for the train. His face was pale, and his eye wild and anxious. "The stage broke down, and I missed the first train," thought he, "and then that boy told me to get out here. I've made a bad beginning and I'm afraid this trip will have a bad ending."

"Allow me to assist you, sir."

There were many passengers walking to and fro on the platform, waiting for the cars to come.

Among them was a plain-featured, honest-looking boy, who had been accompanied to the sration by his mother. Just before she bade him "good-bye," she said, "Lyman, look at that pale, sad old man.

I do n't believe he is used to traveling. Perhaps you can help him along."

As the train came into the station, the lad stepped up to Mr. Randal, and said, respectfully: "Allow me to assist you, sir." Then he took hold of his arm, and guided him into the car to a seat.

"Thank you, my boy. I'm getting old and clumsy, and a little help from a young hand comes timely. Where are you going, if I may ask?"

"To Harrowtown, sir. I saw an advertisement for a boy in a store, and I'm going to try to get the situation. My name is Lyman Dean."

"Ah? I'm sure I wish you success, Lyman, for I believe you 're a good boy. You are going to the same place I am. I want to find Aaron Harrington, but I've had two mishaps. I do n't know what's coming next."

"I'll show you right where his office is. I've been in Harrowtown a good many times."

Half an hour later, the brakeman shouted the name of the station where they must stop. Lyman assisted Mr. Randal off the train, and walked with him to the principal street. "Here's Mr. Harrington's office," said he.

"Oh, yes, thank you kindly. And now could you tell me where Mr. Luke Conway's place of business is?"

"Why, that's the very gentleman I'm going to see," said Lyman. "His place is just round the corner, only two blocks off."

Mr. Randal was deeply interested. He turned

and shook the boy's hand, warmly. " Lyman," he
said, " Mr. Conway knows me. I am going to see
him by-and-by. I am really obliged to you for
your politeness, and wish I could do something for
you. I hope Mr. Conway will give you the situation, for you deserve it. If you apply before I get
there, tell him Gideon Randal is your friend.
Good-by."

Fifteen minutes after found Lyman waiting in
the counting-room of Luke Conway's store. Albert
Gregory had just preceded him. The merchant
was writing, and he had requested the boys to be
seated a short time,
till he was at leisure.
Before he finished his
work, a slow, feeble
step was heard ap-
proaching, and an old
man stood in the door-
way.

"Luke, do n't you
remember me ? " The
merchant looked u p
at the sound of the
voice. Then he sprang
from his chair and
grasped the old man's
hands in both his own.

" Welcome, my benefactor ! "

" Mr. Randal ! Welcome, a thousand times welcome, my benefactor ! " he exclaimed. Seating his
guest, Mr. Conway inquired after his health and

comfort, and talked with him as tenderly as a loving son. It was evident to the quick perception of the merchant that the good old man's circumstances had changed, and he soon made it easy for him to unburden his mind.

"Yes, Luke, I am in trouble. Aaron Harrington owns a mortgage on my farm. I can't pay him, and he threatens to take my home," said Mr. Randal, with a quivering lip. "I went to his office, but did n't find him, and I thought may be you'd advise me what to do."

"Mr. Randal," answered the merchant, laying his hand on the old man's shoulder, "almost thirty years ago when I was cold, and hungry, and friendless, you took me in and fed me. Your good wife —God bless her!—made me a suit of clothes with her own hands. You found me work, and you gave me money when I begun the world alone. Much if not all that I am in life I owe to your sympathy and help, my kind old friend. Now I am rich, and you must let me cancel my debt. I shall pay your mortgage to-day. You shall have your home free again."

Mr. Randal wiped great hot tears from his cheeks, and said, in a husky voice, "It is just as I told Martha. I knew, if we lent our money to the Lord, when a dark day came, He would provide."

The reader can imagine the different feelings of the two boys, as they sat witnesses of the scene. The look of derision, that changed to an expression of sickly dismay, on Albert's face, when the old man came in and was so warmly greeted by the merchant, was curiously suggestive. But his usual assurance soon returned. He thought it unlikely that Mr. Randal would recognize him in the daylight, and he determined to put on a bold front.

For a minute the two men continued in conversation. Mr. Conway called up pleasant reminiscences of "Aunt Martha," his boy-life on the farm, and the peace and stillness of the country town. He thought a railway ride of a hundred miles must be quite a hardship for a quiet old man. "It was a long way for you," he said, "Did you have a comfortable journey?"

"Well, I can't quite say that. First, the stage broke down and delayed me. Then I slept in the cars, and a boy played a trick on me, and waked me up, and made me get out at the wrong station, so I had to stay over nigh in Whipple Village. To tell the truth I had a great deal of worriment with one thing and another, getting here; but it's all right now," he added, with a radiant face.

"Is this the boy who lied to you?"

"You shall go with me to my house and rest, as soon as I have dismissed these boys," said Mr. Conway, earnestly; and turning to Albert and Lyman,

who anxiously waited, he spoke to them about
their errand.

"I suppose you came because you saw my advertisement?"

"Yes, sir," replied both, simultaneously.

"Very well. I believe you came in first," he
began, turning to Albert. "What is your name?"

"I am Albert Gregory, sir. I think I can suit
you. I've brought testimonials of ability and character from some of the first men—Esq. Jenks, Rev.
Joseph Lee, Dr. Henshaw, and others. Here are
my letters of recommendation," holding them out
for Mr. Conway to take.

"I don't care to see them," returned the merchant, coldly. "I have seen you before. I understand your character well enough for the present."

He then addressed a few words to Lyman Dean.

"I should be very glad of work," said Lyman.
"My mother is poor, and I want to earn my living,
but I have n't any testimonials."

"Yes, you have," said old Mr. Randal, who was
waiting for an opportunity to say that very thing.
And then he told the merchant how polite and
helpful Lyman had been to him.

Mr. Conway fixed his eyes severely upon the
other boy. The contrast between him and young
Dean was certainly worth a lesson.

"Albert Gregory," said the merchant, "I occupied the seat in the car in front of you last evening.
I heard you exultingly and wickedly boasting how
you had deceived a distressed and helpless old

man.   Mr. Randal, is this the boy who lied to you,
and caused you to get out at the wrong station?"

"I declare!   Now I do remember him.   It is!
I'm sure it is," exclaimed the old gentleman, fixing
his earnest eyes full upon the crimson face of the
young man.

It was useless for Albert to attempt any vindica-
tion of himself.   His stammered excuses stuck in
his throat, and he was glad to hide his mortification by an early escape.   Crestfallen, he slunk
away, taking all his " testimonials " with him.

"Lyman," said Mr. Conway kindly, "I shall be
very glad to employ you in my store.   You shall
have good pay if you do well, and I am sure you
will.   You may begin work at once."

Lyman's eyes danced with joy as he left the
counting-room to
receive his in-
structions from
the head clerk.

Mr. Conway
furnished the
money to pay the
debt due to Mr.
Harrington by
Mr. Randal,
and a heavy load
was lifted from

Mr. Randal pays
Mr. Harrington.

the good old farmer's heart.   He remained a visitor
two or three days in Mr. Conway's house, where he
was treated with the utmost deference and attention.

Mr. Conway also purchased for him a suit of warm clothes, and an overcoat, and sent his confidential clerk with him on his return journey to see him safely home. Nor was good Mrs. Randal forgotten. She received a handsome present in money from Mr. Conway, and a message full of grateful affection. Nothing ever after occurred to disturb the lives of the aged and worthy pair.

Albert Gregory secured an excellent situation in New York, but his false character, and his wanton disregard of others' feelings and rights, made him as hateful to his employers as to all his associates, and it soon became necessary for him to seek another place.

He has changed places many times since, and his career has been an unhappy one—another example of the results of frivolous habits and a heartless nature.

Lyman Dean is now a successful merchant, a partner of Mr. Conway, and occupies a high position in society, as an honorable, enterprising man. But best of all, he is a Christian, and finds deep satisfaction and happiness in the service of Him who has said: —

"Thou shalt rise up before the hoary head, and honor the face of the old man, and fear thy God."

BERT'S THANKSGIVING

AT noon on a dreary November day, a lonesome little fellow stood at the door of a cheap eating house, in Boston, and offered a solitary copy of a morning paper for sale to the people passing.

But there were really not many people passing, for it was Thanksgiving day, and the shops were shut, and everybody who had a home to go to, and a dinner to eat, seemed to have gone home to eat that dinner.

Bert Hampton, the newsboy, stood trying in vain to sell the last *Extra* left on his hands by the dull business of the morning.

An old man, with a face that looked pinched, and who was dressed in a seedy black coat, stopped at the same doorway, and, with one hand on the latch, he appeared to hesitate between hunger and a sense of poverty, before going in.

It was possible, however, that he was considering whether he could afford himself the indulgence of a morning paper, seeing it was Thanksgiving day; so at least Bert thought, and addressed him accordingly:—

"Buy a paper, sir? All about the fire in East Boston, and arrest of safe-burglars in Springfield. Only two cents."

The little old man looked at the boy, with keen gray eyes which seemed to light up the pinched look of his face, and answered in a shrill voice:—

"You ought to come down in your price, this time of day. You can't expect to sell a morning paper at 12 o'clock for full price."

"Well, give me a cent, then," said Bert. "That's less than cost;

"Buy a paper, sir?"

but never mind. I'm bound to sell out, anyhow."

"You look cold," said the old man.

"Cold," replied Bert, "I'm nearly froze. And I want my dinner. And I'm going to have a big dinner, too, seeing it's Thanksgiving day."

"Ah! lucky for you, my boy!" said the old man. "You've a home to go to, and friends, too I hope."

"No, sir; no home, and no friend—only my mother." Bert hesitated and grew serious, then suddenly changed his tone—"and Hop Houghton. I told him to meet me here, and we'd have a first-rate Thanksgiving dinner together, for it's no fun to be eating alone Thanksgiving day! It sets a fellow thinking,—if he ever had a home, and then has n't got a home any more."

"It's more lonesome not to eat at all," said the old man, his gray eyes twinkling. "And what can a boy like you have to think of? Here, I guess I can find one cent for you—though there's nothing in the paper, I know."

The old man spoke with some feeling, his fingers trembled, and somehow he dropped two cents instead of one into Bert's hand.

"Here! you've made a mistake!" cried Bert. "A bargain's a bargain. You've given me a cent too much!"

"No, I did n't,—I never give anybody a cent too much!"

"But—see here!" And Bert showed the two cents, offering to return one.

"No matter," said the old man. "It will be so much less for *my* dinner—that's all."

Bert had instinctively pocketed the pennies, but his sympathies were excited.

"Poor old man!" he thought; "he's seen better days, I guess. Perhaps he's no home. A boy like me can stand it, but I guess it must be hard for him. He meant to give me the odd cent, all the while; and I do n't believe he has had a decent dinner for many a day."

All this, which I have been obliged to write out slowly in words, went through Bert's mind like a flash. He was a generous little fellow, and any kindness shown him, no matter how trifling, made his heart overflow.

"Look here," he cried; "where are *you* going to get your dinner, to-day?"

"I can get a bite here as well as anywhere—it do n't matter much to me," replied the old man.

"Come; eat dinner with me," said Bert, "I'd like to have you."

"I'm afraid I could n't afford to dine as you are going to," said the man, with a smile, his eyes twinkling again.

"I'll pay for your dinner!" Bert exclaimed. "Come! we do n't have a Thanksgiving but once a year, and a fellow wants a good time then."

"But you are waiting for another boy."

"Oh! Hop Houghton. He won't come now, it's too late. He's gone to a place down in North street, I guess,—a place I do n't like, there's so much tobacco smoked and so much beer drank there." Bert cast a final glance up the street, but could see nothing of his friend.

"No, he won't come now. So much the worse for him! He likes the men down there; I do n't."

"Ah!" said the man, taking off his hat and giving it a brush with his elbow as they entered the restaurant, as if trying to appear as respectable as he could in the eyes of a newsboy of such fastidious tastes.

To make him feel quite comfortable in his mind on that point, Bert hastened to say:—

"I mean rowdies, and such. Poor people, if they behave themselves, are just as respectable to me as rich folks. I ain't at all aristocratic!"

"Ah, indeed!" And the old man smiled again, and seemed to look relieved. "I'm very glad to hear it."

He placed his hat on the floor, and took a seat opposite Bert at a little table which they had all to themselves. Bert offered him the bill of fare.

"I must ask you to choose for me; nothing very extravagant, you know I am used to plain fare."

"So am I. But I'm going to have a dinner, for once in my life, and so are you," cried Bert, generously. "What do you say to chicken soup—and wind up with a big piece of squash pie! How's that for a Thanksgiving dinner?"

"Sumptuous!" said the old man, appearing to glow with the warmth of the room and the prospect of a good dinner. "But won't it cost you too much?"

"Too much? No, sir!" said Bert. "Chicken soup, fifteen cents; pie—they give tremendous big pieces here, thick, I tell you—ten cents. That's twenty-five cents; half a dollar for two. Of course, I don't do this way every day in the year! But mother's glad to have me, once in a while. Here! waiter!" And Bert gave his princely order as if it were no very great thing for a liberal young fellow like him, after all.

"Where is your mother? Why don't you take dinner with her?" the little man asked.

Bert's face grew sober in a moment.

"That's the question! Why don't I? I'll tell you why I don't. I've got the best mother in the world! What I'm trying to do is to make a home for her, so we can live together, and eat our Thanksgiving dinners together, sometime. Some boys want one thing, some another; there's one goes in for good times, another's in such a hurry to get rich, he don't care much how he does it; but what I want most of anything is to be with my mother and my two sisters again, and I am not ashamed to say so."

Bert's eyes grew very tender, and he went on; while his companion across the table watched him with a very gentle, searching look.

"I haven't been with her now for two years— hardly at all since father died. When his business was settled up,—he kept a little hosiery store on Hanover street,—it was found he hadn't left us anything. We had lived pretty well, up to that time, and I and my two sisters had been to school; but then mother had to do something, and her friends got her places to go out nursing; she's a nurse now. Everybody likes her, and she has enough to do. We couldn't be with her, of course. She got us boarded at a good place, but I saw how hard it was going to be for her to support us, so I said, 'I'm a boy; *I* can do something for myself; you just pay the board for the girls and keep

them to school, and I'll go to work, and maybe
help you a little, besides taking care of myself."

"What could you do?" said the little old man.

"That's it; I was only eleven years old; and
what could I do? What I should have liked
would have been some nice place where I could do
light work, and stand a chance of learning a good
business. But beggars mustn't be choosers. I
couldn't find such a place; and I wasn't going to
be loafing about the streets, so I went to selling
newspapers. I've sold newspapers ever since, and
I shall be twelve years old next month."

"You like it?" said the old man.

"I like to get my own living," replied Bert,
proudly. "But what I want is, to learn some
trade, or regular business, and settle down and
make a home for my mother. But there's no use
talking about that.

"Well I've told you about myself," added Bert;
"now suppose *you* tell *me* something?"

"About myself?"

"Yes. I think that would go pretty well with
the pie."

But the man shook his head. "I could go back
and tell you about many of my plans and high
hopes when I was a lad of your age; but it would
be too much like your own story over again. Life
isn't what we think it will be, when we are young.
You'll find that out soon enough. I am all alone
in the world now; and I am nearly seventy years
old."

"It must be so lonely, at your age! What do you do for a living?"

"I have a little place in Devonshire street. My name is Crooker. You'll find me up two flights of stairs, back room at the right. Come and see me, and I'll tell you all about my business and perhaps help you to such a place as you want, for I know several business men. Now do n't fail."

And Mr. Crooker wrote his address, with a little stub of a pencil, on a corner of the newspaper which had led to their acquaintance, tore it off carefully, and gave it to Bert.

Thereupon the latter took a card from his pocket, and handed it across the table to his new friend.

> HERBERT HAMPTON
>
> Dealer in Newspapers

The old man read the card, with his sharp gray eyes, which glowed up funnily at Bert, seeming to say, "Is n't this rather aristocratic for a twelve-year-old news-boy?"

Bert blushed and explained :—

"Got up for me by a printer's boy I know. I

had done some favors for him, and so he made me a few cards. Handy to have sometimes, you know."

"Well, Herbert," said the old man, "I'm glad to make your acquaintance, and I hope you'll come and see me. You'll find me in very humble quarters; but you are not aristocratic, you say. Now won't you let me pay for my dinner? I believe I have money enough. Let me see." And he put his hand in his pocket.

Bert would not hear of such a thing; but walked up to the desk, and settled the bill with the air of a person who did not regard a trifling expense.

When he looked around again, the little old man was gone.

"Now mind; I'll go and see him the first chance I have," said Bert, as he looked at the penciled strip of newspaper margin again before putting it into his pocket.

He then went round to his miserable quarters, in the top of a cheap lodging-house, and prepared himself at once to go and see his mother. He could not afford to ride, and it was a long walk,— at least five miles to the place where his mother was nursing.

On the following Monday, Bert, having a leisure hour, went to call on his new acquaintance in Devonshire street.

Having climbed the two flights, he found the door of the back room at the right ajar, and, looking in, saw Mr. Crooker at a desk, in the act of receiving a roll of money from a well-dressed visitor.

Bert entered unnoticed, and waited till the money was counted and a receipt signed. Then, as the visitor departed, Mr. Crooker

"He saw Mr. Crooker receiving a roll of money."

noticed the lad, offered him a chair, and then turned to place the money in the safe.

"So this is your place of business?" said Bert, glancing about the plain office room. "What do you do here?"

"I buy real estate, sometimes — sell — rent — and so forth."

"Who for?" asked Bert.

"For myself," said the old gentleman, with a smile.

Bert started, perfectly aghast, at this situation. This, then, was the man whom he had invited to dinner and treated so patronizingly the preceding Thursday!

"I—I—I thought—you were a poor man!"

"I am a poor man," said Mr. Crooker, locking his safe. "Money does n't make a man rich. I've money enough. I own houses in the city. They give me something to think of, and so keep me alive. I had truer riches once, but I lost them long ago."

From the way the old man's voice trembled and eyes glistened, Bert thought he must have meant by these riches, the friends he had lost, wife and children, perhaps.

"To think of me inviting you to dinner!" he said, abashed and ashamed.

"It was odd. But it may turn out to have been a lucky circumstance for both of us. I like you. I believe in you, and I've an offer to make you. I want a trusty, bright boy in this office, somebody I can bring up to my business, and leave it with, as I get too old to attend to it myself. What do you say?"

What could Bert say?

Again that afternoon he walked—or rather ran—to his mother; and, after consulting with her, joyfully accepted Mr. Crooker's offer.

Interviews between his mother and his employer followed. The lonely, childless old man, who owned so many houses, wanted a home; and one of these houses he offered to Mrs. Hampton, with ample support for herself and children if she would also make it a home for him.

Of course this proposition was accepted; and

Bert soon had the satisfaction of seeing the great
ambition of his life accomplished. He had employment, which promised to become a profitble business, as indeed it did in a few years. The old man
and the lad proved useful to each other; and,
more than that, he was united once more with his
mother and sisters in a happy home, where he has
since had many Thanksgiving dinners.

"One of these houses he offered to Mrs. Hampton."

THE BOY AND HIS SPARE MOMENTS.

A LEAN, awkward boy came one morning to the door of the principal of a celebrated school, and asked to see him.

The servant eyed his mean clothes, and thinking he looked more like a beggar than anything else, told him to go around to the kitchen.

The boy did as he was bidden, and soon appeared at the back door.

"I should like to see Mr. Brown," said he.

"You want a breakfast, more like," said the servant girl, "and I can give you that without troubling him."

"Thank you," said the boy; "I should have no objection to a bit of bread; but I should like to see Mr. Brown, if he can see me."

"Some old clothes, may be, you want," remarked the servant, again eyeing the boy's patched trousers. "I guess he has none to spare; he gives away a sight;" and without minding the boy's request, she set out some food upon the kitchen table and went about her work.

[58]

"Can I see Mr. Brown?" again asked the boy, after finishing his meal.

"Well, he's in the library; if he must be disturbed, he must; but he does like to be alone sometimes," said the girl, in a peevish tone. She seemed to think it very foolish to admit such an ill-looking fellow into her master's presence. However, she wiped her hands, and bade him follow. Opening the library door, she said:—

"Here's somebody, sir, who is dreadfully anxious to see you, and so I let him in."

I do n't know how the boy introduced himself, or how he opened his business, but I know that after talking awhile, the principal put aside the volume he was studying, took up some Greek books, and began to examine the new-comer. The examination lasted some time. Every question which the principal asked, the boy answered as readily as could be.

"Upon my word," exclaimed the principal, "you certainly do well!" looking at the boy from head to foot, over his spectacles. "Why, my boy, where did you pick up so much?"

"*In my spare moments*," answered the boy.

Here he was, poor, hard-working, with but few opportunities for schooling, yet almost fitted for college, by simply improving his *spare moments*. Truly, are not spare moments the "gold dust of time?" How precious they should be! What account can you give of your spare moments? What can you show for them? Look and see.

"Where did you pick up so much?" "In my spare moments."

This boy can tell you how very much can be laid up by improving them; and there are *many* other boys, I am afraid, in the jail, in the house of correction, in the forecastle of a whale ship, in the gambling house, or in the tippling shop, who, if you should ask them when they began their sinful courses, might answer:—

"In my *spare* moments."

"In my spare moments I gambled for marbles."

"In my spare moments I began to smoke and drink."

"It was in my spare moments that I began to steal chestnuts from the old woman's stand."

"It was in my spare moments that I gathered with wicked associates."

Oh, be very, very careful how you spend your spare moments! Temptation always hunts you out in small seasons like these when you are not busy; he gets into your hearts, if he possibly can, in just such gaps. There he hides himself, planning all sorts of mischief. Take care of your spare moments. "Satan finds some mischief still for idle hands to do."

WILL WINSLOW

WILL WINSLOW was the worst boy in the village; his father's indulgence had spoiled him.

"Don't check the boy," he would say to his mother, "you will crush all the manhood in him."

And so he grew up the terror of his neighbors. The old, the infirm, and the crippled were the especial objects of his vicious merriment.

One poor woman, bent by age and infirmities, he assailed with his ridicule, as she daily went out upon her crutch, to draw water from the well near her house, and just within the playground of the schoolhouse.

"Only look at her," he would say, "isn't she the letter S now, with an extra crook in it?" and his cruel laugh, as he followed closely behind, mocking and mimicking her, called forth from her no rebuke.

One day, however, she turned, and looking at him reproachfully, said:—

"Go home, child, and read the story of Elisha and the two bears out of the wood."

"Shame on you, Will," said Charles Mansfield, "to laugh at her misfortunes! I heard my grandmother say that she became a cripple by lifting her invalid son, and tending him night and day."

"I don't care what made her so," said Will, "but I wouldn't stay among people if I was such a looking thing as that. Do look!"

"Shame!" said Charles; "shame!" echoed each of the boys present. And to show their sympathy, several of them sprang forward to aid the poor woman; but Charles Mansfield, the oldest, and always an example of nobleness and generosity, was the first. "Let me get the water for you, ma'am," and he gently took the bucket from her hand.

Her voice was tremulous and tearful, as she said, "Thank you, my dear boy. God grant that you may never suffer from such infirmities."

"If I should," said Charles, kindly, "it would be the duty, and ought to be the pleasure of young people to assist me. One of us will bring you water every day, and so you need not come for it."

"Yes, so we will," was echoed from lip to lip.

"God bless you! God bless you all." She exclaimed as she wiped away the tears and entered her poor and lonely home.

Will Winslow was reported to the master, and was sentenced to study during the usual recess for a week to come. The punishment was hard, for he

loved play better than his book; but how slight
in comparison with the retribution which awaited
him.

It was the second day of his confinement, and he
sat near the open window, watching
the sports of the boys in the
playground. Suddenly,
when the master was ab-
sorbed in his occupations, he
leaped into the midst of
them, with a shout at his
achievement.

"Now let him punish
me again, if he can," and
he ran backward, throw-
ing up his arms, and shouting in defiance, when
his voice suddenly
ceased; there was a
heavy plunge, and
a horrible groan
broke on the ears of
his bewildered com-
panions.

Now it happened

"There was a heavy plunge, and a groan."

that the well, of which we have before spoken,
was undergoing repairs, and the workmen were
then at a distance collecting their materials. Carelessly the well was left uncovered, and at the very
moment of his triumph, Will Winslow was pre-
cipitated backward into the opening.

A cry of horror burst from the assembled boys, who rushed to the spot, and Charles Mansfield, the bravest of them all, was the first to seize the well-rope, tie it around his waist, and descend to the rescue.

The well was deep; fortunately, however, the water at that time was mostly exhausted, but Will lay motionless at the bottom. Carefully Charles lifted him, and with one arm around his mutilated and apparently lifeless form, and the other upon the rope, he gave the signal, and was slowly drawn to the top.

The livid face of the wicked boy filled his companions with horror; and in perfect silence they bore him to the house of the poor woman, which was close at hand. She had witnessed the accident from the window, and upon her crutch hastened to meet them.

And now Will Winslow was in the humble home, and upon the lowly bed of her whom he had assailed with cruelty and scorn; and faithfully she obeyed the commandment of Him who said: —

"Do good to them that hate you, and pray for them which despitefully use you, and persecute you."

Silently her prayers ascended to God for the sufferer. Her little vials of camphor and other restoratives, provided by charitable neighbors, were emptied for his relief. She took from her scanty store, bandages for his head, which was shockingly mangled and bleeding; and she herself, forgetful of all but his sufferings, sat down and tenderly bathed his hands and his forehead, while some of the boys ran for the surgeon, and others for the master.

The injury to the head was supposed to be the only one he had sustained; and after the surgeon had done his work, the poor boy was borne away on a litter to his home, still insensible, and surrounded by his companions, mute with emotion. That day was destined to make an impression upon the school, its master, and all that heard of the awful catastrophe.

A few hours later and a group of boys collected in the playground. Their conversation was in whispers; horror sat upon every face; all were pale and awe stricken. Charles Mansfield approached.

"How is poor Will now, have you heard?"

"Oh, Charlie!" several exclaimed at once as they gathered around him.

"Oh! don't you know? haven't you heard? Why, he opened his eyes and spoke, but they think his back is broken."

Charles clasped his hands, lifted them high in the air, uttered not a word, but burst into tears. For a few minutes he wept in silence, and then, still pale and grief stricken, but with a manly voice, he said to his companions:—

"Boys, shall we ever forget the lesson of this day?"

And poor Will—words would be too feeble to portray his agony of body and mind as he lay for long months upon his bed of suffering; but when he arose therefrom, with a feeble and distorted body, and a scar upon his forehead, he was changed in heart also, crushed in spirit, humble, and contrite.

Repentance had had its perfect work, and when he became convalescent, and his schoolmates came to congratulate him on his recovery, he threw his arms around the necks of each, and burst into tears, but could not speak, except to whisper, "Forgive, forgive."

At his request the poor woman became the tenant, rent free, of a cottage belonging to his father, and his mother constantly ministered to her wants. As soon as he could do so, he wrote to her, humbly pleading her forgiveness, and in return she gave him her blessing.

From this time one half of his ample quarterly allowance was given her; he visited her in her loneliness, and at last made his peace with God, and declared his punishment just—henceforth to be a cripple and a hunchback.

Youthful readers, let the history of Will Winslow impress your hearts. Revere the aged, whether they be in poverty or affluence; and feel it a privilege to minister to them in their infirmities, as they have done to you in the weakness and helplessness of infancy. It is the only recompense which youth can make to age, and God will bless the youthful heart which bows in reverence before the hoary head.

ONLY THIS ONCE

I'LL be in again very soon, mother; I am only going 'round the corner to see the new billiard rooms;" and, cap in hand, Harry was closing the parlor door when his mother called him back.

"I cannot consent to your going there, my dear," she said; "you must know that both your father and myself disapprove of all such places."

"But I don't intend to play, mother; only to look on; the boys say the tables are splendid; and besides, what could I tell Jim Ward after promising to go with him? He is waiting outside for me. Please say 'yes' only this once."

"Tell Jim that we rather you would remain at home; and ask him to walk in and spend the evening," said Harry's father, as he looked up from the paper.

"Oh, I know he'll not do that!" and Harry stood turning the door handle, till, finding that his parents did not intend to say anything more, he walked slowly to the front step.

"Why don't you hurry along," called Jim, "and not keep a fellow standing all night in the cold?"

"I am not going. Won't you come in?" said Harry.

[68]

"Not going! Your mother surely does n't object to your looking at a billiard table!"

"She would prefer I should not go," said Harry, and Jim's only reply was a significant whistle, as he walked off.

"He'll be sure to tell all the boys!" said Harry, half aloud, as he shut the front door with rather more force than was necessary. "I do n't see what

"I wonder if my son feels too old for a story?"

does make father and mother so particular." Then, entering the parlor, he took the first book that came to hand from the table, and, taking a seat very far from the light, looked exceedingly unamiable.

His father laid aside the paper, and without seeming to notice Harry's mood, said pleasantly, "I wonder if my son feels himself too old for a story; if not I have one to tell him which might well be named, 'Only This Once.'" The book was returned to the table; but Harry still kept thinking of what the boys would say when Jim told an exaggerated story, and his countenance remained unchanged.

"When I was about your age, Harry," began his father, "we lived next door to Mr. Allen, a very wealthy gentleman, who had one son. As Frank was a good-natured, merry boy, and had his two beautiful ponies, several dogs, and a large playground, he soon made friends.

"Many an afternoon did we spend together, riding the ponies, or playing ball on the playground, and one summer afternoon in particular, I never expect to forget, for it seems to me now, looking back upon it, as the turning point of Frank's life; but we little thought of such a thing at the time.

"It was a very warm afternoon; and, becoming tired of playing ball, we had stopped to rest on the piazza, when Frank proposed that we should take the ponies to a plank road a few miles from the house, and race them. I was certain that his father would disapprove of this, and, besides, it would have been most cruel work on such a warm afternoon, so I tried to make Frank think of something else he would like to do instead; but all in vain.

"'I think you might go, Charlie,' he said. 'What's the harm of doing it; *only this once?* I just want to see if either of my ponies is likely to be a fast trotter.'

"For one moment I hesitated, but in the next came the thought of my father's displeasure, and I shook my head.

"'Very well, just as you please, Mr. Good Boy! I know plenty who will be glad of the chance to ride Jet;' and so saying he walked away.

"Frank did find a boy who was delighted to go with him, and enjoyed the race so much that, notwithstanding his father's reprimand, he managed to pursue the same sport more times than 'only that once.'

"As soon as the summer was ended, Mr. Allen went to Europe for his health, and I did not see his son again for three years, till I left the country and entered the same college with him.

Frank began studying very earnestly; but before the first year was ended, the earnestness had passed away. Friends would induce him to spend his evenings at their rooms, or at some

"Only this once."

public place of amusement, and each time Frank would try to satisfy his conscience with, 'It will be only this once.'

"Thus by degrees, his lessons were neglected, and as study became irksome, his love for excitement and gaiety increased, till one day I overheard a gentleman, who knew him well, remark that he feared Frank's 'only this once' would prove his ruin.

"But a few years before, Frank would have been shocked with the thought of spending the afternoons in racing, and evenings in billiard saloons. He had not at first really intended to visit these places more than 'once,' 'just to see for myself;' but there are very few who ever stop in the course of wrong doing at 'only this once.'

"At length his father died. When the sad tidings reached the son, he seemed more thoughtful for a time; but in an hour of temptation he yielded. Before long his old companions surrounded him again, and of them he soon learned how to spend the large fortune left him by his father, in a most reckless manner.

"In vain his true friends tried to check him in his wild career; and, five years ago, Harry, my poor friend Frank died a drunkard."

"Oh, father, how dreadful!" and Harry shuddered.

"Yes, it is dreadful, my son; but there are countless untold stories as dreadful as this one. If we were to visit a prison, and ask the wretched inmates how it was that they were first led into crime, we should find that '*only this once*' brought most of them there. One took something which did not belong to him, never intending to do it more than that once; but the crime soon grew into a habit. Another was once tempted to gamble, and only that one game was the foundation of all his crimes. Another fully intended to stop with the first glass; but instead, became a reckless drunkard.

"Learn, my son, to dread those three little words, and when tempted to use them, think of all they may lead to, and ask for strength to resist the temptation; and, Harry, do you wonder now at our refusing to allow you to visit the billiard room even once?"

"No, father; I see now that you were right, and I was wrong in supposing that it could not possibly do me any harm to go only this once; and if Jim *does* tell the boys some silly story to make them laugh at me, I can tell them about Frank Allen, and that will soon sober them."

My dear boys, do you flatter yourself that it is a trifling thing to do wrong, "only this once?" If so, stop and consider, how often not only the young but those of mature years yield to to this deceptive and alluring thought and take the first steps in a career of sin, when, could they but see the end of the path which they are so thoughtlessly entering, they would shudder with horror. They do not realize that sin once indulged in hardens the heart, and that one step in the downward path leads to the broad road.

How many parents yield to the pleadings of their children to be indulged "this once," who find that to deny after once being indulged, costs a greater effort than to have stood with firmness to conviction of conscience and true principle.

THE RIGHT DECISION

IT was the beginning of vacation when Mr. Davis,
a friend of my father, came to see us, and
asked to let me go home with him. I was much
pleased with the thought of going out of town.

The journey was delightful, and when we reached
Mr. Davis's house everything looked as if I were
going to have a fine time. Fred Davis, a boy
about my own age, took me cordially by the hand,
and all the family soon seemed like old friends.

"This is going to be a vacation worth having,"
I said to myself several times during the evening,
as we all played games, told riddles, and laughed
and chatted merrily.

At last Mrs. Davis said it was almost bedtime.
Then I expected family prayers, but we were very
soon directed to our chambers. How strange it
seemed to me, for I had never before been in a
household without the family altar.

"Come," said Fred, "mother says you and I are
going to be bed fellows," and I followed him up
two pair of stairs to a nice little chamber which he
called his room. He opened a drawer and showed
me a box, and boat, and knives, and powderhorn,

[74]

and all his treasures, and told me a world of new things about what the boys did there.

Then he undressed first and jumped into bed. I was much longer about it, for a new set of thoughts began to rise in my mind.

When my mother put my purse into my hand, just before the train started, she said tenderly, in a low tone, " Remember, Robert, that you are a Christian boy."

I knew very well what that meant, and I had now just come to a point of time when her words were to be minded.

At home I was taught the duties of a Christian child; abroad I must not neglect them, and one of these was evening prayer. From a very little boy I had been in the habit of kneeling and asking the forgiveness of God, for Jesus' sake, acknowledging His mercies, and seeking His protection and blessing.

" Why don't you come to bed, Robert?" cried Fred. " What are you sitting there for?"

I was afraid to pray, and afraid not to pray. It seemed that I could not kneel down and pray before Fred. What would he say? Would he not laugh? The fear of Fred made me a coward. Yet I could not lie down on a prayerless bed. If I needed the protection of my heavenly Father at home, how much more abroad.

I wished many wishes; that I had slept alone, that Fred would go to sleep, or something else, I hardly knew what. But Fred would not go to sleep.

Perhaps struggles like these take place in the bosom of every boy when he leaves home and begins to act for himself, and on his decision may depend his character for time, and for eternity. With me the struggle was severe.

At last, to Fred's cry, "Come, boy, come to bed,"

"I will kneel down and pray first."

I mustered courage to say, "I will kneel down and pray first; that is always my custom." "Pray?" said Fred, turning himself over on his pillow and saying no more.

His propriety of conduct made me ashamed. Here I had long been afraid of him, and yet when he knew my wishes, he was quiet and left me to myself. How thankful I was that duty and conscience triumphed.

That settled my future course. It gave me strength for time to come. I believe that the decision of the "Christian boy," by God's blessing, made me a Christian man; for in after years I was thrown amid trials and temptations which must have drawn me away from God and from virtue, had it not been for my settled habit of secret prayer.

Let every boy who has pious parents, read and think about this. You have been trained in Christian duties and principles. When you go from home, do not leave them behind.

Carry them with you, and stand by them; then, in weakness and temptation, by the help of God, they will stand by you.

Take your place like a man, on the side of your God and Saviour, of your mother's God and Saviour, and of your father's God.

It is by a failure to do this, that so many boys go astray, and grow up to be young men dishonoring their parents, without hope and without God in the world.

ASHAMED of Jesus! that dear friend,
On whom my hopes of heaven depend?
No; when I blush, be this my shame,
That I no more revere His name.

Ashamed of Jesus! yes, I may,
When I've no guilt to wash away,
No tears to wipe, no good to crave,
No fears to quell, no soul to save.

"Herbert closed his book and began playing with some marbles."

THE USE OF LEARNING

I am tired of going to school," said Herbert Allen to William Wheeler, the boy who sat next to him. "I do n't see any great use, for my part, in studying geometry, and navigation, and surveying, and mensuration, and the dozen other things that I am expected to learn. They will never do me any good. I am not going to get my living as a surveyor, or measurer, or sea captain."

"How are you going to get your living, Herbert?" his young friend asked, in a quiet tone, as he looked up into his face.

"Why, I am going to learn a trade; or, at least, my father says that I am."

"And so am I," replied William; "and yet my father wishes me to learn everything that I can; for he says that it will all be useful some time or other in my life."

"I'm sure I can't see what use I am ever going to make, as a saddler, of algebra or surveying."

"Still, if we can't see it, Herbert, perhaps our fathers can, for they are older and wiser than we are. And we ought to try to learn, simply because

[78]

they wish us to, even if we do not see clearly the use in everything that we are expected to study."

"I can't feel so," Herbert replied, tossing his head, "and I do n't believe that my father sees any more clearly than I do the use of all this."

"You are wrong to talk so," protested his friend, in a serious tone. "I would not think as you do for the world. My father knows what is best for me, and your father knows what is best for you; and if we do not study and improve our time, we will surely go wrong."

"I am not afraid," responded Herbert, closing the book which he had been reluctantly studying for half an hour, in the vain effort to fix a lesson on his unwilling memory. Then taking some marbles from his pocket, he began to amuse himself with them, at the same time concealing them from the teacher.

William said no more, but turned to his lesson with an earnest attention. The difference in the character of the two boys is plainly indicated in this brief conversation. To their teacher it was evident in numerous particulars — in their conduct, their habits, and their manners. William always recited his lessons correctly, while Herbert never learned a lesson well. One was always punctual at school, the other a loiterer by the way. William's books were well taken care of, Herbert's were soiled, torn, disfigured, and broken.

Thus they began life. The one obedient, industrious, attentive to the precepts of those who were older and wiser, and willing to be guided by them ; the other indolent, and inclined to follow the leadings of his own will. Now, at the age of thirty-five, Mr. Wheeler is an intelligent merchant, in an active business ; while Mr. Allen is a journeyman

"The contrast in their appearance was very great."

mechanic, poor, in embarrassed circumstances, and possessing but a small share of general information.

"How do you do, my old friend?" said the merchant to the mechanic, about this time, as the latter entered the counting room of the former. The contrast in their appearance was very great. The merchant was well dressed, and had a cheerful look ; while the other was poorly clad, and seemed troubled and dejected.

"I cannot say that I do very well, Mr. Wheeler," the mechanic replied, in a tone of despondency. "Work is very dull, and wages low ; and, with so large a family as I have, it is tough enough getting along under the best circumstances."

" I am really sorry to hear you say so," replied the merchant, in a kind tone. " How much can you earn now ? "

" If I had steady work, I could make twelve or fifteen dollars a week. But our business is very bad. The consequence is, that I do not average nine dollars a week, the year round."

" How large is your family ? "

" I have five children, sir."

" Five children ! And only nine dollars a week ! "

" That is all, sir; but nine dollars a week will not support them, and I am, in consequence, going behindhand."

" You ought to try to get into some other business."

" But I do n't know any other."

The merchant mused awhile, and then said: " Perhaps I can aid you into getting into something better. I am president of a newly-projected railroad, and we are about putting on the line a company of engineers, for the purpose of surveying and locating the route. You studied surveying and engineering at the same time I did, and I suppose have still a correct knowledge of both; if so, I will use my influence to have you appointed surveyor. The engineer is already chosen, and you shall have time to revive your early knowledge of these matters. The salary is one hundred dollars a month."

A shadow, still darker than that which had
before rested there, fell upon the face of the mechanic.

"But," he said, "I have not the slightest knowledge of surveying. It is true I studied it, or rather
pretended to study it, at school; but it made no
permanent impression on my mind. I saw no use
in it then, and am now as ignorant of surveying as
if I had never taken a lesson on the subject."

"I am sorry, my old friend," replied the merchant. "But you are a good accountant, I suppose, and I might, perhaps, get you into a store.
What is your capacity in this respect?"

"I ought to have been a good accountant, for I
studied mathematics long enough; but I took little
interest in figures, and now, although I was for
many months, while at school, pretending to study
bookkeeping, I am utterly incapable of taking
charge of a set of books."

"Such being the case, Mr. Allen, I really do not
know what I can do for you. But stay; I am
about sending an assorted cargo to Buenos Ayres,
and thence to Callao, and want a man to go as
supercargo, who can speak the Spanish language.
The captain will direct the sales. I remember that
we studied Spanish together. Would you be willing to leave your family and go? The wages will
be one hundred dollars a month."

"I have forgotten all my Spanish, sir. I did not
see the use of it while at school, and therefore it
made no impression upon my mind."

After thinking a moment, the merchant replied : —

"I can think of but one thing that you can do, Mr. Allen, and that will not be much better than your present employment. It is a service for which ordinary laborers are employed, that of chain carrying for the surveyor to the proposed railroad expedition."

"What are the wages, sir?"

"Forty dollars a month."

"And found?"

"Certainly."

"I will accept it, sir, thankfully," the man said. "It will be much better than my present employment."

"Then make yourself ready at once, for the company will start in a week."

"I will be ready, sir," the poor man replied, and then withdrew.

In a week the company of engineers started, and Mr. Allen with them as a chain carrier, when, had he, as a boy, taken the advice of his parents and friends, and stored his mind with useful knowledge, he might have filled the surveyor's office at more than double the wages paid to him as chain carrier. Indeed, we cannot tell how high a position of usefulness and profit he might have held, had he improved all the opportunities afforded him in youth. But he perceived the use and value of learning when it was too late.

I hope that none of my young readers will make

the same discovery that Mr. Allen did, when it is too late to reap any real benefit. Children and youth cannot possibly know as well as their parents, guardians, and teachers, what is best for them. They should, therefore, be obedient and willing to learn, even if they cannot see of what use learning will be to them.

"It is chain carrying for the surveyor."

JAMIE AND HIS TEACHER

AMONG the scholars in a mission Sabbath school formed in one of our large country villages, was a little Irish boy, whose bright, intelligent face, quickness of mind, and earnest attention to the lessons, had awakened great interest in the mind of his teacher.

After a few Sabbaths, however, this boy was missing, and when sought by the visiting committee during the week, was never to be found.

Sometimes he was seen from a distance, looking with apparent interest, as the superintendent or one of the teachers passed by, but if they attempted to approach him, he would take to his heels, and spring over walls and fences with such agility that there was no hope of overtaking him.

Miss L., his teacher in the Sabbath school, was a young lady belonging to one of the wealthiest families in the village. One cold afternoon in December, after Jamie had been absent from his class more than a month, he made his appearance at the back door of her father's house, asking to see her.

"No, no," said the cook, "ye need n't be thinking the young leddy'll come in the woodshed to see ye. If ye have any message, ye can go in the house."

"I don't look nice enough to go in," said Jamie, glancing ruefully at his torn trousers and coarse, muddy boots.

But it so happened that Miss L. was passing through the hall, and she heard and recognized the voice at once; so she came to the door to see what was wanted.

Jamie hung his head in confusion, while the young lady kindly took his hand in hers, and asked if he had been well, and why he had not been to Sabbath school.

"Me father wouldn't let me come," he sobbed out at last; "he bate me because I'd been to the Sabbath school."

"Poor child!" exclaimed Miss L. "But does your father know you came here this afternoon?"

"No, ma'am; but he said I might have every half holiday to go skating, if I promised never to go inside the Sabbath school again. So I brought me Testament, and I thought mebbe you'd teach me here, ma'am."

Was it not a bold request? Did not Jamie know that with home duties and the claims of social life, his teacher's time must be fully occupied? Might she not think that her services on the Sabbath were all that should be required of her?

Ah, no; what were time, and strength, and fashionable amusements, to be compared with the value of a precious soul? Miss L. could only thank God

for so rich a privilege, and enter with joy upon the
work of instruction.

So every half holiday found Jamie seated by her
side in the beautiful library, earnestly studying the
words of the Master, who has said, "Suffer little
children to come unto Me."

Skating-time came and went; the last
ice had melted from the pond; but never
once had Jamie gone skating.   He had
found a
source of bet-
ter, deeper
delight, than
even boyish
sports could
afford.

But Jamie
could not al-
ways hide the
fact that he
was spending

"It's me Testament, father."

his time in this way.

One day, his well-worn Testament fell from his
pocket in the presence of his parents.

"What's that?" demanded the father fiercely.

"It's me Testament, father," Jamie gently
replied.

"And where did ye get that?   Have ye been to
the Sabbath school since I told ye not?"

"No, father; but my teacher gave me this a
great while ago."

" And who is your teacher? "

" Miss L."

" What, Miss L.? The one that lives in that splendid house on the hill? "

" Yes, father."

" Well, well, what's in the book? let's hear a bit."

Providentially, this was one of the rare occasions

"What's in the book? let's hear a bit."

when Mr. Ryan was not intoxicated, and as the boy read passage after passage from his beloved book, the father's mind opened with a child-like interest to the truths of the holy word.

From that day he became a sincere inquirer after the truth as it is in Jesus. The appetite for strong drink, which had been the cause of his degradation, was at last quenched; for a stronger thirst had taken possession of his soul, even for that purifying stream of which whosoever drinketh shall never thirst.

When sober, Mr. Ryan was an industrious and intelligent man, and by his renewed energies his family was soon placed in a position of comfort and respectability. But that was not all the good effect of Jamie's love for the truth.

Within a few months, both father and mother had cast off the fetters of restraint, and were receiving for themselves with meekness and earnestness, that precious word which was able to save their souls.

Had not Jamie made the very best use of his winter holidays? and was not his teacher richly rewarded for all her exertions?

How many of our young readers will study with equal earnestness the word of truth, which is always open to them, that they may learn from it the way of life? How many Christian teachers will engage with equal interest in the work of instruction, in the hope that in so doing they may save a soul from death?

HOSANNA to the Son
   Of David and of God,
Who brought the news of pardon down,
   And bought it with His blood.

To Christ the anointed King
   Be endless blessings given;
Let the whole earth His glories sing,
   Who made our peace with heaven.

"WITH A WILL, JOE!"

IT was a summer afternoon; the wheelbarrow stood before Mrs. Robbins' door; the street was empty of all traffic, for the heat was intense.

I sauntered languidly along on the shady side opposite the widow's house, and noticed her boy bringing out some linen in a basket, to put on the wheelbarrow.

I was surprised at the size of the basket he was lugging along the passage and lifting on to the wheelbarrow, and paused to look at him. He pulled, and dragged, and then resting a moment began again, and in the silence of the street, I heard him saying something to himself.

I half crossed the road. He was too busy to notice me, and then, in a pause of his toil, I heard him gasp out: —

"With a will, Joe!" He was encouraging himself to a further effort with these words. At last, bringing the large basket to the curbstone, he ran in and got a piece of smooth wood as a lever; resting one end of the basket on the wheelbarrow, he heaved up the other end, and saying a little louder than before, "With a will, Joe," the basket was mounted on to the wheelbarrow.

As he rested, and looked proudly at his successful effort, he saw me, and his round, red face, cov-

"I've managed it, mother."

ered with perspiration, became scarlet for a moment, as I said:—

"That's a brave boy." The mother's voice sounded in the passage:—

"I'm coming, Joe!" and out she came, as the child, pointing to the basket, exclaimed:—

"I've managed it, mother!" It was a pretty sight,—the gratified smile of the widowed mother, as she fondly regarded her willing boy. Though no further word was spoken, the expression of satisfaction on their faces was very plain, and I have no doubt in each heart there was a throb of pleasure for which words have no language.

I went on my way, but the saying, "With a will,

Joe," went with me. How much there was in that simple phrase, " With a will! "

How different is our work according as we do it with or against our will. This little fellow might have cried or murmured, or left his mother to do the work, and been dissatisfied with himself, and a source of discontent to his mother; but he had spurred himself on to toil and duty, with his words, powerful in their simplicity—" With a will, Joe."

Often since have I recalled the scene and the saying. When some young lady complains to me, " I have no time to give to doing good. I've visits to make, and shopping to do, and embroidery to finish, how can I help the poor when I'm so pressed for time?" I am apt to say mentally, " How different it would be with her, if she had ever said to herself, ' With a will.' "

Yes, with a will we can do almost anything that ought to be done; and without a will we can do nothing as it should be done. To all of us, whatever our station, there come difficulties and trials. If we yield to them, we are beaten down and conquered.

But if we, ourselves, conquer the temptation to do wrong, calling the strength of God to aid us in our struggle with the enemy, we shall grow stronger and more valiant with every battle, and less liable to fall again into temptation. Our wisdom and our duty are to rouse ourselves,—to speak to our own hearts as the child did in his simple words, " With a will, Joe."

"I shan't go to school."

EFFECTS OF DISOBEDIENCE

THE following affecting narrative was related by a father to his son, as a warning, from his own bitter experience of the sin of resisting a mother's love and counsel.

What agony was on my mother's face when all that she had said and suffered failed to move me. She rose to go home and I followed at a distance. She spoke to me no more until she reached her own door.

"It is school time now," she said. "Go, my son, and once more let me beseech you to think upon what I have said."

"I shan't go to school," said I.

She looked astonished at my boldness, but replied firmly:—

"Certainly you will, Alfred! I command you!"

"I will not," said I.

"One of two things you must do, Alfred—either go to school this minute, or I will lock you up in your room, and keep you there until you promise implicit obedience to my wishes in the future."

[93]

"I dare you to do it," I said; "you can't get me up stairs."

"Alfred, choose now," said my mother, who laid her hand upon my arm. She trembled violently and was deadly pale.

"If you touch me, I will kick you!" said I in a

"Take this boy up stairs and lock him in his room."

fearful rage. God knows I knew not what I said.

"Will you go, Alfred?"

"No," I replied, but I quailed beneath her eyes.

"Then follow me," said she as she grasped my arm firmly. I raised my foot,—O, my son, hear me,—I raised my foot and kicked her—my sainted mother! How my head reels as the torrent of memory rushes over me. I kicked my mother, a feeble woman—my mother. She staggered back a few steps and leaned against the wall. She did not look at me.

"O, heavenly Father," she cried, "forgive him, he knows not what he does." The gardener, just then passing the door, and seeing my mother pale and almost unable to support herself, came in.

"Take this boy up stairs and lock him in his room," said she, and turned from me. She gave me a look of agony, mingled with most intense love, from a true and tender heart that was broken.

In a moment I found myself a prisoner in my own room. I thought for a moment I would fling myself from the open window, but I felt that I was afraid to die. I was not penitent. At times my heart was subdued, but my stubbornness rose in an instant, and bade me not yield yet.

"It was my sister."

The pale face of my mother haunted me. I flung myself on my bed and fell asleep. Just at twilight I heard a footstep approach my door. It was my sister.

"What shall I tell mother for you?" she said.

"Nothing," I replied.

"O, Alfred, for my sake and for all our sakes, say that you are sorry. She longs to forgive you."

I would not answer. I heard her footsteps slowly retreating, and flung myself on the bed to pass a wretched night.

Another footstep, slower and more feeble than my sister's, disturbed me. "Alfred, my son, shall I come in?" she asked.

I cannot tell what influence made me speak adverse to my feelings. The gentle voice of my mother, that thrilled me, melted the ice from my heart, and I longed to throw myself upon her neck; but I did not. My words gave the lie to my heart when I said I was not sorry. I heard her withdraw. I heard her groan. I longed to call her back, but I did not.

I was awakened from an uneasy slumber by hearing my name called loudly, and my sister stood by my bedside:—

"Get up, Alfred! Do n't wait a minute. Get up and come with me, mother is dying!"

I thought I was yet dreaming, but I got up mechanically, and followed my sister. On the bed, pale as marble, lay my mother. She was not yet undressed. She had thrown herself upon the bed to rest, and rising again to go to me she was seized with heart failure, and borne to her room.

I cannot tell you my agony as I looked upon
her,—my remorse was tenfold more bitter from the
thought that she never would know it. I believed
myself to be her murderer. I fell on the bed beside
her ; I could not weep. My heart burned within
me; my brain was on fire. My sister threw her
arms around me and wept in silence. Suddenly
we saw a motion of mother's hand ; her eyes un-
closed. She had recovered her consciousness, but
not her speech.

"Mother, mother!" I shrieked; "say only that
you forgive me."

She could not speak, but her hand pressed mine.
She looked upon me, and lifting her thin, white
hands, she clasped my own within them, and cast
her eyes upward. She moved her lips in prayer,
and thus died. I remained kneeling beside that
dear form till my sister removed me ; but the joy of
youth had left me forever.

Boys who spurn a mother's counsel, who are
ashamed to own that they are wrong, who think it
manly to resist her authority, or yield to her influence, beware. One act of disobedience may
cause a blot that a life-time can not wipe out.
Wrong words and wrong actions make wounds that
leave their scars.

Be warned; subdue the first rising of temper,
and give not utterance to the bitter thought. Shun
the fearful effects of disobedience. Lay not up for
yourselves sad memories for future years.

The Shipwreck

STAND BY THE SHIP

"DO, grandmother, tell us about the little drummer boy whose motto was, 'Stand by the ship.'"

"Grandmother is not used to telling children stories; but, if you will be quiet, she will try." And this is the story she told us:—

During one of the fiercest battles of the civil war, the colonel of a Michigan regiment noticed a very small boy, acting as drummer.

The great coolness and self-possession of the boy, as displayed during the engagement; his habitual reserve, so singular in one of his years; his orderly conduct, and his fond devotion to his drum (his only companion, except a few well-worn books),— all these things unusual in one so young had attracted notice, both from the officers and the men. Colonel B.'s curiosity was aroused, and he desired to know more of him. So he ordered that the boy should be sent to his tent.

The little fellow came, his drum on his breast, and the sticks in his hands. He paused before the

The Drummer Boy in Battle

colonel and made his best military salute.   He was a noble looking boy, the sunburnt tint of his face in good keeping with his dark, crisp curls.

But strangely out of keeping with the rounded cheeks and dimpled chin, was the look of gravity and thoughtfulness, in the serious, childish eyes. He was a boy, who seemed to have been prematurely taught the self-reliance of a man.   A strange thrill went through Colonel B.'s heart as the boy stood before him.

"Come forward, I wish to talk to you."   The boy stepped forward, showing no surprise under the novel position in which he found himself.   "I was very much pleased with your conduct yesterday," said the colonel, "from the fact that you are so young and small for your position."

"Thank you, colonel ; I only did my duty ; I am big enough for that, if I *am* small," replied the noble little fellow.

"Were you not very much frightened when the battle began?" questioned Colonel B.

"I might have been, if I had let myself think of it ; but I kept my mind on my drum.   I went in to play for the men ; it was that I volunteered for. So I said to myself : 'Don't trouble yourself about what doesn't concern you, Jack, but do your duty, and stand by the ship.'"

"Why, that is sailors' talk," said the colonel.

"It is a very good saying, if it is, sir," said Jack.

"I see you understand the meaning of it.   Let

that rule guide you through life, and you will gain the respect of all good men."

"Father Jack told me that, when he taught me to say, 'Stand by the ship.'"

"He was your father?"

"No, sir,—I never had a father,—but he brought me up."

"Strange," said the colonel, musing, "how much I feel like befriending this child. Tell me your story, Jack."

"I will tell it, sir, as near as I can, as Father Jack told it to me.

"My mother sailed on a merchant ship from France to Baltimore, where my father was living. A great storm arose; the ship was driven on rocks, where she split, and all hands had to take to the boats. They gave themselves up for lost; but at last a ship bound for Liverpool took them up. They had lost everything but the clothes they had on; but the captain was very kind to them; he gave them clothes, and some money.

"My mother refused to remain at Liverpool, though she was quite sick, for she wanted to get to this country so badly; so she took passage in another merchant ship, just going to New York. She was the only woman on board. She grew worse after the ship sailed; the sailors took care of her. Father Jack was a sailor on this ship, and he pitied her very much, and he did all he could for her. But she died and left me, an infant.

"Nobody knew what to do with me; they all

said I would die—all but Father Jack; he asked the doctor to give me to him. The doctor said:—

"'Let him try his hand, if he has a mind to; it's no use, the little one will be sure to go overboard after its mother;' but the doctor was wrong.

"*I went errands for gentlemen, and swept out offices and stores.*"

"I was brought safe to New York. He tried to find my father, but did not know how to do it, for no one knew my mother's name. At last he left me with a family in New York, and he went to sea again; but he never could find out anything about my mother, although he inquired in Liverpool and elsewhere. The last time he went to sea, I was nine years old, and he gave me a present on my birthday, the day before he sailed. It was the last; he never came back again; he died of ship fever.

"But Father Jack did well by me; he had me placed in a free school, at seven years of age, and always paid my board in advance for a year.

"So you see, sir, I had a fair start to help myself, which I did right off.   I went errands for gentlemen, and swept out offices and stores.   No one
liked to begin with me, for
they all thought me too small,
but they soon saw I got along
well enough.

"I went to
school just the
same, for I did
my jobs before
nine in the morning; and
after school closed at night, I
had plenty of time to work
and learn my lessons.   I
wouldn't give up my school,
for Father Jack told me to
learn all I could, and some
day I would find my father,
and he must not find me a
poor, ignorant boy.   He said
I must look my father in the
face, and say to him without
falsehood: 'Father, I may be
poor and rough, but I have
always been an honest boy
and stood by the ship, so you
need n't be ashamed of me.'   Sir, I could never
forget those words."   He dropped his cap, drum,
and sticks, bared his little arm, and showed the

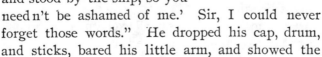

figure of a ship in full sail, with this motto beneath
it, pricked into the skin : "Stand by the ship."

"When I was twelve, I left New York and came
to Detroit with a gentleman in the book business.
I was there two years, when the war broke out.

"One day, a few months afterward I was passing by a recruiting office, and went in. I heard
them say they wanted a drummer. I offered; they
laughed and said I was too little; but they brought
me a drum and I beat it for them. They agreed
to take me. So the old stars and stripes was the
ship for me to stand by."

The colonel was silent; he seemed to be in deep
thought. "How do you ever expect," he said, "to
find your father? You do not even know his
name."

"I do n't know, sir, but I am sure I shall find
him, somehow. My father will be certain to know
that I am the right boy, when he does find me, for
I have something to show him that was my
mother's," and he drew forth a little canvas bag,
sewed tightly all around, and suspended from his
neck by a string.

"In this," he said, "is a pretty bracelet that my
mother always wore on her arm. Father Jack took
it off after she died, to keep for me. He said I
must never open it until I found my father, and
that I must wear it so around my neck, that it
might be safe."

"A bracelet, did you say?" exclaimed the colonel,
"let me have it — I must see it at once!"

With both his small hands clasped around it, the little boy stood looking into Colonel B.'s face; then, slipping the string from over his head, he silently placed it in his hand. To rip open the canvas was but the work of a moment.

"I think I know this bracelet," stammered Colonel B. "If it be as I hope and believe, within the locket we will find two names, —*Wilhelmina and Carleton; date, May 26, 1849.*"

There were the names as he said. Colonel B. clasped the boy to his heart, crying brokenly, "My son! my son!"

I must now go back in my story. In the first year of his married life, Colonel B. and

"He silently placed it in his hand."

his lovely young wife sailed for Europe, expecting to remain several years in Southern Europe, on account of the delicate health of his wife.   He was engaged in merchandise in the city of Baltimore. The sudden death of his business partner compelled his return to America, leaving his wife with her mother in Italy.

Soon after he left, his mother-in-law died.   Mrs. B. then prepared to return to Baltimore at once, and took passage on the ill-fated steamer which was lost.   Vainly he made inquiries ; no tidings came of her.   At last he gave her up as dead ; he almost lost his reason from grief and doubt.

Fourteen years had passed ; he did not know that God in his mercy had spared to him a precious link with the young life so lost and mourned. Restless, and almost aimless, he removed to Michigan.   When the war broke out, he was among the first to join the army.

There stood the boy, tears streaming down his cheeks.   "Father," he said, "you have found me at last, just as Father Jack said.   You are a great gentleman, while I am only a poor drummer boy. But I have been an honest boy, and tried my best to do what was right.   You won't be ashamed of me, father?"

"I am proud to call you my son, and thank God for bringing you to me just as you are."

My little hero is now a grown man ; and as the boy was so is the man.   "Stand by the ship," the motto which served him so well while a boy, is his motto still.

A FAITHFUL SHEPHERD BOY

GERHARDT was a German shepherd boy, and a noble fellow he was, although he was very poor.

One day he was watching his flock, which was feeding in a valley on the borders of a forest, when a hunter came out of the woods and asked:—

"How far is it to the nearest village?"

"Six miles, sir," replied the boy; "but the road is only a sheep track, and very easily missed."

The hunter looked at the crooked track and said:—

"My lad, I am very hungry and thirsty; I have lost my companions and missed my way; leave your sheep and show me the road. I will pay you well."

"I cannot leave my sheep, sir," replied Gerhardt. "They will stray into the forest, and may be eaten by wolves or stolen by robbers."

"Well, what of that?" queried the hunter. "They are not your sheep. The loss of one or more would n't be much to your master, and I'll give you more than you have earned in a whole year."

"I cannot go, sir," rejoined Gerhardt, very firmly. "My master pays me for my time, and he trusts me with his sheep; if I were to sell my time, which does not belong to me, and the sheep should get lost, it would be the same as if I stole them."

"Well," said the hunter, "will you trust your sheep with me while you go to the village and get some food, drink, and a guide? I will take care of them for you."

The boy shook his head. "The sheep do not know your voice, and—" he stopped speaking.

"And what? Can't you trust me? Do I look like a dishonest man?" asked the hunter, angrily.

"Sir," said the boy, "you tried to make me false to my trust, and wanted me to break my word to my master; how do I know that you would keep your word to me?"

The hunter laughed, for he felt that the lad had fairly cornered him. He said:—

"I see, my lad, that you are a good, faithful boy. I will not forget you. Show me the road and I will try to make it out myself."

Gerhardt then offered the contents of his bag to the hungry man, who, coarse as it was, ate it gladly. Presently his attendants came up, and then Gerhardt, to his surprise, found that the hunter was the grand duke, who owned all the country round.

The duke was so pleased with the boy's honesty, that he sent for him shortly after that, and had him educated.

In after years Gerhardt became a great and powerful man, but he remained honest and true to his
dying day.

"Presently his attendants came up."

DICK HARRIS; OR, THE BOY-MAN

DICK HARRIS was called a clever boy, and no one believed this more firmly than he. He was only fourteen years of age, and yet he dearly loved to be thought a man.

As he was about to leave school, his friends often asked him what he intended to be. Dick could not tell; only, that it must be something great. Now while Dick had learned some good thing in school, he had also learned many evil habits — among them the practice of smoking.

Dick's father smoked. He saw men smoking in the streets, and so he thought it would be manly to smoke. Along with some of his schoolmates, he used to hide himself and take his turn of the one pipe or cigar which they had among them. As they were afraid of being found out, they hid the pipe when any one came near.

His father, who although he smoked himself, forbade Dick doing so, asked him one day why his clothes smelled so of tobacco smoke.

"Some of my schoolmates smoke, father."

"But do you smoke?"

"No."

"Take care you do n't then; it's all very well for men, but I won't have any of my children smoking."

Dick went away, as the Bible says, "with a lie in his right hand."

And yet he wanted to be a man. Now look at that, my lads. What is it that makes a man—I mean a true man? There are many things. The Bible says that the glory of young men is their strength—strength of body, and strength of mind.

Would Dick get this kind of glory by smoking? He certainly would not strengthen his body, for it has been proved again and again that boys who smoke weaken their bodies.

Tobacco is a poison—slower perhaps than strong drink, but quite as sure; and although it may not kill you outright, because the quantity taken is not large enough, yet it pollutes the blood, injures the brain and stomach, and paralyzes many of the healthy functions of the body.

The result is stunted growth and general weakness. A boy who smokes much never can have the glory of bodily strength.

Dick found this out for himself, to his bitter regret. And besides this, do you think that his conduct showed strength of mind? He began the practice of smoking, not because he believed it to be right, but because *men* smoked. He was only a boy, yet he wished to appear *a man*—that is, to appear what he was *not*.

What could be more weak than for a boy to have
no reason for doing a thing than that *men do it?*
But it led to something worse. He was smoking
on the sly, and to conceal it he became a liar. He
lied in the school by his conduct, he lied at home
by his words.

We could have respected him, although we

*"Became the associate of fast
young men and learned to drink."*

pitied him, had he smoked
openly and taken the con-
sequences ; but who can re-
spect a coward? He is not worthy of the name of
man. Dick continued to smoke after he left
school, and was apprenticed in a large warehouse.
Here again the old desire to be like men in-
fluenced him. They had cigars, he must have
one ; they smoked, he must do so. This conduct
had its invariable effects. He became the associate
of "fast" young men—got into debt—learned to
drink—stayed out late at night—and before his
apprenticeship had ended, was ruined in health ;

and but for the indulgence of his employers would
have been discharged in disgrace. Was that acting
the part of a man?

This happened many years ago. Last week
amidst a crowd who surrounded a polling booth,
there stood a man about forty years of age—he
looked twenty years older. On his head was a bat-
tered hat; he wore a seedy, black coat; both his
hands were in his pockets, and in his mouth the
stump of a cigar which had been half-smoked by
another man; his face was bloated, his eyes bleared
and languid. Even the vulgar crowd looked at
him with contempt.

I looked into his face thinking there was in it a
resemblance to one I had known. Slowly and
painfully came the sad truth, that the drunken
creature was Dick Harris; he had become a man
but he was a lost man.

It has often been said, "How great a matter a
little fire kindleth." The spark which kindled a
blaze among Dick's evil passions, was the spark
which lit the tobacco pipe at school. Bad habits
are easily acquired, but they are hard to get rid of.
See what smoking had done for Dick. It led him
to drink, and the two habits have left him a
wreck.

But you say to me, "There are many thousands
who smoke, and yet are strong men." It is so.
But in almost all cases these strong smokers did
not begin the habit while they were boys; if they
had done so, the likelihood is, they never would

"The drunken creature was Dick Harris."

have become strong men. Besides, how much stronger they might have been if they had never smoked!

Many who smoke and still appear strong, have nevertheless undermined their constitution, and when an unusual strain comes upon it there is a collapse.

"But again," you say, "all who smoke do not learn to drink, and so lose true manhood." That may be; and yet there is a significant fact that a confirmed drunkard who does not smoke can scarcely be found. It has recently been shown that the great majority of those who break their temperance pledge are smokers.

Smoking and drinking are branches of the same deadly tree whose leaves curse the nation.

And now, my lads, "Quit you like men, be strong." The next time any one says to you, "Have a cigar," say "No!"

If he says it is manly to smoke, say "No; it is manly to exercise self-control; to act from principle; to have cleanly habits; to be unselfish; to pay one's debts; to be sober; and to have the approval of one's conscience. Now, I might lose all these elements of manhood if I learned to smoke."

THE WAY OF SAFETY.

 EAR grandma is one of those who "being
dead yet speaketh."

She was not a preacher, or a lecturer — much
less a censurer or reprover; but she was that most
agreeable of teachers to childhood and youth, a
story-teller. Yet, let no one suppose that she told
us tales of fairy lore or ingenious romance, as per-
nicious as they are false. Not so; the stories to
which we listened with so much delight, were all
true, and all from the capacious store-house of her
own memory.

We had returned from the church one Sabbath
afternoon, and as usual, hastened to grandma to
repeat as much as we could remember of the sermon. The text was that solemn command of the
wise man: "My son, if sinners entice thee, consent thou not;" and our pastor had made it the
ground-work of a powerful exhortation to the young
especially, to beware of the many temptations,
snares, and allurements which they should meet;
and warned them of the consequences of yielding

to the seductive influences by which they might be surrounded.

"That reminds me of a young man whom I knew before any of you were born," grandma remarked, when we had reported as much as we could remember of the sermon. "You have heard me speak of Jacob Wise?" she said, addressing my father.

"Yes, mother," he replied, "please tell the children about him. I am sure your account of his experience will be a very suitable addition to our afternoon sermon."

"O yes, grandma, please do!" we exclaimed; and, drawing our seats around her, we prepared for what we knew would be a treat. The good old lady did not need to be urged, but, after pausing a moment to collect her thoughts, began as follows: —

"Jacob Wise was the son of a near neighbor when I was a happy wife in my Western home. His father was a plain, practical man, respected for his uprightness, good sense, and piety; and he brought up his son in his own sound principles, at the same time giving him all the education that was within his reach.

"When Jacob was about fourteen years of age, he was sent to Louisville for the benefit of a year's instruction in a large school there.

"There were, also, other sons and daughters around his father's hearth. It therefore appeared expedient that Jacob should be allowed to develop his taste for commercial pursuits.

"The first circumstances of any note, that I remember, which particularly marked his character, occurred at the time of his first practical acquaintance with business.

"While in Louisville, he received much attention from the family of a wealthy man who kept a large store in the city; and when, at the close of his school term, he was offered a place behind the counter of his friend, he found no difficulty in obtaining his father's permission to accept of it.

"The merchant, Mr. Rankin, was a smooth, bland, good-tempered man, and in his intercourse with the world maintained outwardly a fair and honest character.

"But Jacob had not been many weeks in intimate connection with him before he discovered that his dealings were not all conducted with scrupulous adherence to divine law; neither was a conscientious regard to his neighbor's interests a very deepseated principle. This caused the lad much uneasiness; and a feeling of nervous disquiet took possession of the hitherto happy boy.

"He hesitated as to which was the more honorable course: to obey his employer without question, or to sacrifice his own ideas of strict integrity.

"But he was not long left in doubt. One day a carriage drove to the door, and a richly dressed lady entered the store, and asked to be shown some children's necklaces. Jacob, who attended in that

department, was proceeding to wait on her, when
Mr. Rankin came forward smiling, and with the
ease and courtesy for which he was noted, took the
lad's place, and spread before the lady an assort-
ment of glittering trinkets which, judging from her
gay appearance,
he knew would
please her eye.

An animated
dialogue ensued
between the mer-

*" To all this Jacob
listened with
grief and as-
tonishment."*

chant and his customer,
respecting the style and
value of the various ar-
ticles under view. The lady was made to believe
that this elegant display had been imported with
great cost and difficulty from the manufacturing
cities of Europe, and, in consequence of the im-

mense and rapid demand for them, the obliging trader had been satisfied with moderate profit, and was now willing to dispose of the remainder of the stock at fabulously low prices.

"To all this, which he knew to be utterly and  shamelessly false, Jacob listened with equal grief and astonishment, and it was with difficulty that he restrained his honest indignation as he saw one after another of the tinsel gewgaws transferred to the shopping bag of the deceived customer at prices which were five times their value, while she was duped with the flattering persuasion that she was receiving unequaled bargains.

"Thought it quite impossible that they could agree."

"All doubts as to the unlawfulness of his remaining another hour under the roof where this swindling transaction had taken place, were immediately removed from the mind of the noble and upright youth.

"When Mr. Rankin returned after having very politely attended the lady to her carriage, and placed the parcel containing her purchases by her side, he was met by Jacob, who, with an air of grave rebuke rarely assumed by lads of his years, informed him that from what he had seen of his method of conducting business he thought it quite impossible that they could agree.

"He was, therefore, resolved to return without delay to his father's house, and he was glad that the terms upon which he had entered the establishment left him free to do so.

"The firm and fearless bearing of the boy awed the man of unjust practices, and he neither attempted to vindicate his own meanness nor to oppose the departure of his right-minded assistant. At once Jacob returned to the old homestead, his character more permanently formed by the ordeal through which he had passed."

"But do you think, grandma," inquired Henry, "that Jacob would have acted so independently if he had had no home to return to?"

"Yes, dear, I think he would," was the prompt reply. "He had learned to obey the commands of God and to believe His promises. He knew that the injunction, 'Come out from among them,' was followed by the assurance, 'I will receive you,' and such was his trust in his heavenly Father's word that no thought for his future provision would have interfered with the performance of what he deemed to be his duty."

"Well, grandma," said Henry, "I like the stand taken by the honest boy. Please go on with the story."

"Jacob remained at home for the next three years, making himself useful in teaching his younger brothers and sisters, besides assisting his father in the management of his affairs. In the meantime his own education was advancing. Nor was he without receiving many offers of clerkship in the neighboring cities, whither the good report of his honesty and integrity had come.

"But a cousin of his father, who was a merchant of some eminence in New Orleans, had proposed to take him into his counting house in a confidential capacity when he should reach a more mature age, and for this important post he was qualifying himself.

"Accordingly, when he was eighteen years of age, at the request of his relative, he again left home. This time his departure was a more serious affair than it had been when, a few years before, he left for school in Louisville.

"Now he was going to a large and populous city, where fashion and vice walked hand in hand, and where snares and pitfalls were spread for the simple and unwary, with scarcely a finger-mark cautioning them to beware.

"All the neighborhood was moved with anxiety and friendly interest for the youth, and the last Sabbath of his attendance at our rural church, the good pastor made an earnest and affectionate address from the same text which the minister presented to-day.

"Our friend's journey to the great maritime city of the South was not without incident. Mr. Wise accompanied his son to Louisville, and, after the necessary preliminary arrangements, went with him on board the boat that was to bear him down the broad waters of the Mississippi.

"The parting advice and benediction of his father were then given. He reminded him of the subject of his pastor's last sermon, and closed by giving him, as the motto of his life, the imperative charge, 'Come out from among them.'

"Then, as he desired to return home by daylight, and the boat was not to start for a couple of hours, he once more committed his son to the care and guidance of heaven, and left him, with a calm trust that he would be kept in the way of safety.

"After a pleasant trip on board the 'Southern Belle,' our young friend arrived in New Orleans.

"Jacob was much pleased with his new situation. He found his relative a man of the most honorable character. Accommodations were procured for him in a first-class boarding-house, where none but persons of the best standing were admitted. And, whether owing to his attractions of mind or person, the sterling worth of his character, or the independent position of his family, or perhaps all these combined, he soon found himself an object of marked interest and attention to all with whom he came in contact.

The Steamboat Trip Down the Mississippi

[124]

"Naturally of a social disposition, and disposed to look at everything in the most favorable light, Jacob saw none of those vicious traits and habits which he had been cautioned to shun.

"He did not partake of the mirthful spirit by which the unwary are enticed into scenes of folly, neither did he deny himself innocent recreations.

"And now to the unsophisticated youth, life presented the fairest aspect. His religious duties were carefully attended to, and in the faithful discharge of his business engagements no one could be more careful and punctual. His evenings were devoted to the society of those who were congenial to him. But it was not long before the hidden thorns of the flowers that strewed his path began to make themselves felt, nor was it without pain that conscience awoke him from the repose in which he had been lulling himself.

"Among the many charming sojourners at the establishment in which he had taken up his abode, was the family of a wealthy planter, who had come to the city for the winter. Mr. and Mrs. De Veaux were a lively and fashionable couple, and their children partook of the gay and careless temperament of their parents.

"Isabel, the eldest, was now in her sixteenth year, and the faultless beauty of her face and figure was only equaled by the child-like sweetness of her disposition. She had been brought up without much restriction or control, and now that she was entering society for the first time, being gay, spirited, and witty, she flung herself into the enjoyments of fashionable pleasure with all the zest of her nature.

"The winter glided along with its witching gayeties, and, though the young Christian was never tempted to join the giddy multitude in their unlawful pastimes, yet his views were more lax than they had been.

"With the hope of his presence having a restraining effect upon the fair being who had touched the tenderest chords of his nature, he suffered himself to be led into scenes such as sober conscience could not approve.

"At length, however, the alarm came that was to disturb his security. A sermon was to be preached by a celebrated minister before the members of the 'Young Men's Christian Association.' Jacob attended, and heard with startled interest the minister deliver, as his text, the very same verse which the pious pastor of his country home had made the subject of the last discourse he had heard from him: 'My son, when sinners entice thee consent thou not.'

"The young man of irreproachable life had no idea that this exhortation could be applied to his case; he had been careful that 'sinners' were granted no opportunity of enticing him.

"But to many of the young men present, who were not so cautious, he hoped the sermon would prove of benefit. So he settled himself comfortably to listen to the brilliant orator.

"But his self-complacency did not last long. It

was that very class to which he belonged, that the
preacher addressed. He exposed the cunning temptations of Satan, and told how he labored to lead
even those who hated vice, to join in the pleasures
of the world, without requiring them to commit
one apparent sin.

"Thus the enemy sought to lead even the Christian, and to turn his heart from God, from holiness,
and from heaven.

"Painfully solemn were the feelings with which
Jacob left the house of God at the close of the service. The film had passed from his eyes, and he
saw that while his outward walk had been strictly
correct, his heart had wandered from its true al
legiance.

"When he reached home he found a gay party
of young people, dancing and making merry in the
brilliantly lighted parlors. But the sickening sen-
sations that ran through his frame, at the thought
of time thus wasted, and creatures fashioned in
their Maker's image perverting their fine intelli-
gences, showed the change that had been made in
his views within the last hour.

"He went at once to his chamber, and with
earnest prayer, he gave himself anew to his Master.

"He decided at once that Isabel must be given
up, with all her attractions. How lone and cheer-
less the future appeared. Casting himself upon
his knees, he prayed for help to bear the blow
which had descended upon his hopes.

"With Jacob Wise, to know his duty was to do

it.   Having felt the evil influence of intimate association with light and giddy worldlings, he determined to change his boarding place to some more
retired spot where no similar temptation should
waylay him.   And so, the next morning, he called

"The next morning he called on his Pastor."

on his pastor, stated the circumstances in which he
was placed, and asked his help in obtaining board
in some private family connected with the church.

"The minister sympathized with his young
friend, and after a few minutes' thought, mentioned
a pious couple of his charge, whose only son had
lately gone from home, and into whose vacant
room he thought it likely Jacob might be admitted.

"It was as he had hoped.   When Mrs. Bennet
heard the case, she was glad to be able to give a
home to the young man.   No other difficulty now
remained but his parting with Isabel.

"He found her seated at the piano, and a long conversation ensued, in which opinions and sentiments entirely opposite were maintained by each. On subjects of vital importance they were disagreed. So that finally they, whose hearts had received their first tender impressions from each other, with an apparent calmness inconsistent with their true feelings, separated, to meet no more."

Grandma paused, and for several minutes no one seemed disposed to speak. Each of us was looking into his own heart to see if there were grace enough there to bear us conquerors through such trials as might be in store for us. The silence was broken by Henry, inquiring the sequel of the young Christian's career.

"Well," said grandma, "Jacob continued to live a consistent, Christian life. He visited his parents every summer, gladdening their hearts by the purity and simplicity of his life.

"When he had been six or seven years in New Orleans, he was taken into partnership by his kinsman and employer; and shortly after he married the daughter of his pastor, whose sweet companionship was a great help to him in his Christian life.

"It is a long time since I have had an opportunity of hearing of Jacob Wise; but I dare say, if still living, he is an example of moral dignity, truth, and uprightness, and an honor to the church of which he has been, from childhood, a steady and consistent member."

ROGER'S LESSON

HURRAH! hurrah! Such a splendid morning for skating; clear as jelly and as cold as ice cream. Come ahead, boys; there's no telling how long this weather will last."

So said Roger to his two friends, whom he met on his way to the park. His eyes sparkled, his cheeks were almost as bright as the scarlet muffler he wore around his neck, and the dangling skates told for themselves the expedition upon which he was bound. The other boys readily agreed to join him, and after running home for their skates, the party started off in such high spirits that the conductor of the car which they entered, begged them to be a little more quiet.

"Not quite so noisy, please, young gentlemen," he said, as they paid their fare.

"Pshaw!" said Roger, while Bob made a face when his back was turned to them, giving Frank an opportunity of noticing the large patch on his overcoat. He made some funny speech about it, at which the others laughed heartily. It usually does boys good to laugh, unless the laugh be at the expense of some one else. A good-natured laugh is good for the heart.

After a while the car stopped for anothor passenger; the conductor assisted the person in getting on, and Roger, thinking more time was taken than usual, called out:—

"Hurry up, hurry up—no time to lose!"

The new-comer was a boy about his own age, but sadly deformed; he was a hunchback, and had a pale, delicate face, which spoke of sorrow and painful suffering.

"Now do move up," said the conductor, as the boys sat still, not offering to make room; but when he spoke, they all crowded together, giving much more room than was necessary,—the three together trying to occupy the space that one would comfortably fill. They continued talking and joking noisily, until the car stopped at the entrance of the park.

Bob and Frank pushed out ahead of all the other passengers. Roger was pushing out after them when the conductor laid his hand on his shoulder.

"Don't crowd, don't crowd; plenty of time, young man."

This expostulation came too late, for Roger in his impatience to get out, unheeding of what he was doing, caught one of his skates in the scarf of the crippled boy, who had been sitting next to him. He gave his skate strap a rude pull, knocking the boy rather roughly, and stepping on a lady's toes.

"Bother take it!" he exclaimed impatiently, and giving the scarf another jerk, ruder than before, he succeeded in disentangling it; then he rushed out, hurried over to the boys who awaited him on the pavement, where they stood stamping their feet and whistling. Roger made no reply to the crippled boy, who said to him gently:—

"It was n't my fault, was it?"

"It was n't my fault, was it?"

"That hunchback caught his scarf in my skate. I thought it never would come out," he exclaimed. "It's kept me all this time!"

"Hush, Roger," interrupted Frank in a low tone of voice.

The boy was just behind them; he had evidently heard what had been said, for his pale face turned scarlet, and lingering behind to see which path the boys intended taking, he walked off in the opposite direction, and they soon lost sight of him.

Roger was hasty and impulsive, but his nature was kindly, after all; and when his skates were fairly on, the ice tried, and the first excitement of the pleasure over, he thought of his unfeeling speech, and the pale, sad face of the boy rose before him.

"Was it my fault?" The question rang in his ears. Was it the boy's fault that his legs were crooked, and his back misshapen and awkward? Was it his fault that he must go through life, receiving pity or contempt from his more fortunate fellow-creatures, whose limbs were better formed than his own?

The more Roger thought, the ruder his treatment of the poor lad now seemed, and putting himself in the boy's place, he felt that such words would have cut him to the quick.

"I say," said Bob, who had been cutting his initials on a smooth, glassy spot of ice: "I say, Roger, what makes you so glum? Why, I declare, there's the little hunchback sitting over there on the bank, looking at the skaters."

Roger looked in that direction, and saw him sitting alone, his only enjoyment consisting in seeing without at all engaging in the pleasure of others.

"What can a poor fellow like that do with himself I wonder?" added Bob. "I don't suppose he can skate or do anything else without making a show of himself."

"That's so," said Roger thoughtfully, wondering how he could make up for his rudeness, or take back his own words. He concluded to let it all pass for this time. In future he would be more careful, and less hasty in speaking; for Roger did not have sufficient manliness to go over to where the boy was sitting, and say frankly; "I beg your pardon for my rudeness."

The boys proposed a game of tag. Roger was a splendid skater; he engaged in the game with great zest: his spirits rose, and the crippled boy and the reproaches of his conscience passed entirely out of his mind as he skated on, knowing that he could keep his balance as well and strike out, perhaps, better than any fellow on the pond.

The swiftest and strongest, however, are not always the most successful, and as he swooped around, curving in very near the shore, a strap gave way, and before Roger could help himself, it tripped him, and he sprawled at full length on the ice.

The boys shouted; some laughed, but a fall is such a common occurrence that no one was very much concerned until Roger attempted to spring up again, to show them all that he did n't mind it in the least,—he would be all right again in a minute. Then he tried to stand; but when an awful pain shot up from his ankle, then he realized that it was quite impossible to stand.

They ran to his assistance, but before they reached him, a soft hand was held out to him, and a gentle voice asked:

"Have you hurt yourself badly?"

Roger saw the deformed boy standing by his side, and then remembered that he had seen him sitting near by on the bank.

"I think I must have sprained my ankle," he replied.

The deformed boy knelt on the ice, and while

"The deformed boy knelt on the ice."

the others clustered around, asking questions and offering suggestions, he quietly unbuckled his skates for him.

"I'll have to get home, I suppose," said Roger faintly; "but, boys, don't let this spoil your fun — don't come with me."

"May I go with you?" said the deformed boy. "I am not going to stay here any longer."

Roger thanked him, and a policeman coming up at that moment to inquire about the accident, a carriage was procured, Roger was put in, the deformed boy followed, and Roger was driven home.

"My fun is spoiled for this winter," he said, with a moan. "I know a fellow who sprained his ankle last year, and the doctor says perhaps he will never be able to skate again. What an unlucky thing for me!—it was n't my fault either."

"No," added the deformed boy gently. "It was not your fault; and it was not my fault that my nurse let me fall when I was a baby and injured my back. I sometimes think it would have been better if she had killed me outright, though strong and well-formed people think it wicked for me to wish that."

The color which had left Roger's pale cheeks from his pain, rushed back for a moment, as he held out his hand and said:—

"I was a brute to you in the car this morning, but I did n't think what I was doing. Will you excuse me?"

"I know you did n't. Please do n't say anything more about it. It is hard to pity the suffering of others unless we have felt pain ourselves."

Roger's sprain prevented him from skating again that season, and taught him also a lesson which let us hope he will remember all his lifetime.

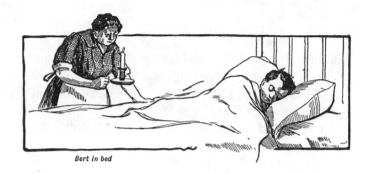

Bert in bed

BERT'S MONITORS

BERT was determined to go. He would n't ask his father, for he was very sure his father would say, No. He did n't quite like to disobey a positive command, so he would say nothing at all about the matter.

Bert was thirteen years old, and it was high time that he began to exercise his own judgment, at least when his own affairs were concerned,— so Bert thought.

He would like to know what harm his going down to the river for a quiet moonlight swim could possibly do to anybody. He would try it, at all events. Ned Sellars would be there, and Frank Peters. They did n't seem to care whether their parents liked it or not. Bert could n't feel so, exactly; but, still, where was the sense in a boy's going to his father every time he turned round?

He was going. He had fully made up his mind to that. He went up to bed at the usual time, however, but his mother coming into his little bedroom about half an hour afterward, was surprised to

find him almost hidden by blanket and quilt, though
it was a warm night in August.

"Why, Bert, you'll smother.   Do let me pull off
some of these clothes."

But Bert held them tightly down.   "I ain't cold,
mother.   I mean I ain't warm."

"Are you sick?"

"No'm."

"Two blankets and a quilt," laughed his mother,
as she turned away.   "I don't know what you're
made of, Bert."

"And jacket and pants and stockings and shoes,"
thought Bert, as he snapped his fingers very softly
under the weight of bedclothes.

The beautiful moon looked in at the little window.   There had been times when Bert, gazing at
her pure, pale face, had marveled that any boy
could have the heart to do wrong when her soft
light was shining on him; but to-night she seemed
to say, "Come on, come on.   I tell no tales.   The
night indoors is warm and stifling.   The river is
cool and clear.   My beams are there before you.
Come on, come on!"

It seemed as if the hours had never lagged so
heavily.   Eleven o'clock was the time agreed upon.

Twice Bert found himself napping.   Suppose he
should go to sleep.   The idea was not to be enter-
tained for a moment.   He sat up in the bed and
listened, listened, listened, until at length the welcome strokes greeted his ear.   He was tired and
sleepy and stupid and very warm.   He opened his

door softly, and went down stairs. He did not dare
unlock the front door, for grandpa's room was just
across the hall, and grandpa
always slept with one eye open.
He crept through the kitchen,
and found himself in the shed.
Was ever anything more fortunate? The outer
door was open.

He took his hat
from the nail, and
just then a plaint-
ive "mew" greeted his ear.

"Hush! Be still, Cuff,"
said he, in a whisper.

But Cuff wouldn't be still.
She was very glad to see
him, and was determined to
tell him so.

"Mew, me-aw," called
Billy, the mocking-bird,
from his cage above.

"Dear me," thought
Bert, "they'll wake
father up as sure as the
world."

*"He opened the door softly,
and went down stairs."*

But it was not unusual
for Billy to sing in the
night. Indeed, his midnight music was sometimes
overpowering. Bert stood very still for a moment,
but could hear no one stirring. He walked on a

The Cat

few steps, Cuff purring loudly, and rubbing her soft gray sides against him.

"Bow, wow, wow, wow," barked the faithful watch-dog.

"Be quiet, Prince. Stop your noise!"

Prince knew his young master's voice, and, like Cuff, was delighted to be near him, and so gave expression to his feelings in a succession of loud quick barks.

"Had n't you better go down, John?" asked Bert's mother, anxiously. "I'm afraid some one is trying to get in."

"They can't get farther than the shed," was the careless reply. "I left that open."

In a few moments all was quiet again. Prince lay down at Bert's feet, and Cuff stretched herself out beside him. Time was pas-

"Me-aw," called Billy.

sing. The boys would surely be there before him. Very carefully he crept toward the door, hardly daring to breathe, in his anxiety.

But Prince had not been asleep. No, indeed! He started up at the first sound of his

"Bow, wow, wow."

master's footsteps. It was very evident that something unusual was going on, and he was determined
to be "in it."

"I must run as fast as I can," said Bert to himself. "Hit or miss, there's nothing else for me to
do."

He was preparing to suit the action to the word,
when Snow, the old family horse, who for a few
days past had been allowed to wander about among
the clover fields, put her
white nose just inside the
door and gave a loud and
fiercely prolonged neigh.

"What next!" muttered
Bert, between his teeth.
"I shall expect to see some
of the cows soon. I don't
care if all the animals on
the place come,—I'm go-
ing."

"The old family horse."

He was walking defiantly from the door, when
he heard his mother's voice at her window. "I
never can sleep, John, with a horse crying around.
I wish you'd go down to see what the trouble is.
And do lock the shed door. I have n't slept five
minutes to-night."

What was Bert to do now? To go forward in
the moonlight, with his mother watching from
above, would be foolish, indeed. To remain in the
shed, to be discovered by his father, seemed equally
unwise.

"Bert came into the shed, and watched his father as he mended an old harness."

He had very little time to think about the matter, for at that moment he heard the well-known footsteps on the stairs. He darted over to the shed closet, shut the door, and tremblingly awaited the result.

And the result was that, after standing painfully still for about ten minutes, during which Prince's significant sniffs and growls had thrice driven him to the very verge of disclosure, he was left unmolested in the dark old closet. He opened the door; but the shed seemed darker yet. No loving cat or friendly dog was there to cheer or to betray. Nothing but thick, black darkness. Was it possible that the moon was still shining outside?

He wondered if the boys were having a good time. He would open the door and go to them as soon as he dared. But while he was thinking and wondering, waiting until he was sure his father and mother were asleep again, the old clock rang out the hour of twelve. Midnight! It was of no use to go then; the boys would be gone.

And so Bert crept up stairs to his room, cross and dissatisfied, feeling that the fates were against him.

He was late to breakfast the next morning. His mother laughingly inquired if the weight of his bedclothes had affected his hearing.

"Yes'm—no'm. I mean—I guess not," he replied absently.

It was a rainy morning, and the weather was disagreeably warm. After breakfast Bert came into the shed, and watched his father as he mended an old harness.

"What sort of boy is that Ned Sellars?" inquired his father at length.

Bert started.

"I don't know. I think he's a pretty good boy. Why?"

"I passed the house this morning. Some one was getting a terrible flogging, and I think it must have been Ned."

"What for? Do you know?"

"Yes. They spoke very loud, and I could n't help hearing. It was for running off last night. Going swimming, I believe."

Bert's eyes flashed.

"That's just like his father," said he, indignantly. "He never wants Ned to have any fun."

There was no reply. Some hidden feeling, he could hardly tell what, prompted Bert's next question.

"Would you

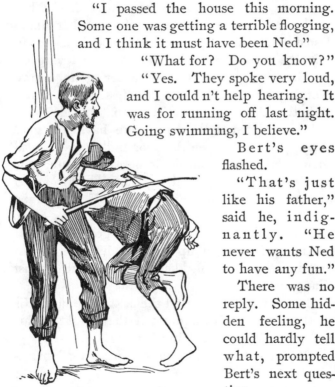

"Some one was getting a terrible flogging."

flog me, father, if I went swimming without leave?"

"That depends upon circumstances," replied his father, looking searchingly into his face. "If my boy was mean enough to skulk out of the house at night, when I supposed him to be abed and asleep, it is just possible that I might not consider him worth flogging."

How Bert's cheeks burned. He had never looked at the matter in just that light before. "*Never* be a sneak, my son. It is cowardly and disgraceful."

Bert made no answer, but his thoughts were busy. Was he not every whit as mean and cowardly as if he had really gone with his unfortunate friend? Yes, verily.

And then he thought of his father. How *good* he was — never denying him any reasonable pleasure; nay, often denying himself for his sake. Bert seemed to realize his father's goodness now as never before.

As he thought of this two large tears rolled down his sunburnt cheeks.

"What is it, my boy?"

He brushed them away hastily.

"Father," said he, "I've been a sneak; but I *won't* be a coward. I was going with the boys last night."

"Ah!"

"Yes. I should have gone if it hadn't been for the dog, and the cat, and—all the rest of them. 'Twasn't any goodness of mine that kept me at home."

His father was silent.

"I wish you'd say something, father," cried poor Bert, impatiently. "I s'pose you do n't think I'm worth flogging; but"—

"My dear boy," said his father, "I knew your footsteps in the shed last night. I knew perfectly well who was hidden in the old closet."

"Why did n't you say so?" inquired astonished Bert, tremblingly.

"Because I preferred to let you go. I thought, if my boy wanted to deceive me, he should, at least, imagine that he had that pleasure."

"O father!"

"Yes, you should have gone, Bert. Very likely I might have gone with you; but you would not have known it."

Bert had n't a word to say.

"I pitied you, too. I knew that, after the fun was over, there must come the settling with your conscience. I was sure you had a conscience, Bert."

The boy tried to speak, but no words came.

"I was disappointed in you, Bert. I was very much disappointed in you."

Down went Bert's head into his hands.

"But now," continued his father, placing one hand upon his shoulder, "now I have my honest boy again, and I am proud of him. I do consider you worth a dozen floggings, Bert; but I have no disposition to give them to you."

Bert wrung his father's hand and rushed out

into the rain. Cuff came running to meet him, and Prince barked with pleasure at his approach. Billy whistled and sung in his cage above, and old Snow's voice was heard in the field close by.

Bert loved them and they knew it. It was some minutes, however, before he noticed them now; and when he did, it was not in his accustomed merry way.

"Just like the monitors at school," said he, seriously. "Making such a fuss that a fellow can't go wrong, if he wants to." And he took Cuff up in his lap, and patted Prince's shaggy coat.

Bert's monitors still watch him with affectionate interest; but never again, I am happy to say, has he felt the least inclination to disturb their midnight slumbers.

A MORNING THOUGHT

WITH every rising of the sun
Think of your life as just begun.

The past has shrivelled and buried deep,
All yesterdays. There let them sleep,

Nor seek to summon back one ghost
Of that innumerable host.

Concern yourself with but to-day,
Woo it, and teach it to obey

Your will and wish. Since time began
To-day has been the friend of man;

But in his blindness and his sorrow
He looks to yesterday and to-morrow.

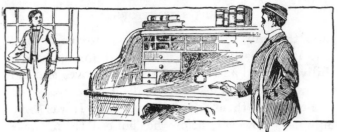

"Laid the pile of bills on the counting room desk."

THE TWO CLERKS

BOYS are apt to think that their parents and teachers are too strict; that they ought not to be obliged to get such perfect lessons, or to go to Sabbath school, to be so punctual and so particular. They wonder why they are not allowed a great many amusements and indulgences which they would like so much.

"What's the use?" they often discontentedly ask.

Well, boys, there is a *great deal* of use in being brought up right; and the discipline which sometimes seems to you so hard, is precisely what your parents see that you need in order to make you worth anything. I will tell you an incident, to illustrate it, which has just come to my knowledge.

William was the oldest child of a widowed mother, and she looked upon him, under God, as her future staff and support. He was trained to industrious habits, and in the fear of God. The day-school and Sabbath school seldom saw his seat vacant. Idleness, that rust which eats into character, had no opportunity to fasten upon him.

By and by he got through school and succeeded in securing a situation in a store in the city.

William soon found himself in quite altered circumstances; the stir and bustle of the streets was very unlike the quiet of his village home; then the tall stores, loft upon loft, piled with goods—boxes and bales now, instead of books and bat; the strange faces of the clerks, and the easy manners and handsome appearance of the rich boy, Ashton, just above him in the store,—all these contributed not a little to his sense of the newness and strangeness of his position.

William looked at Ashton almost with admiration, and thought how new and awkward everything was to himself, and how tired he got standing so many hours on duty, and crowding his way through the busy thoroughfares. But his good habits soon made him many friends. The older clerks liked his obliging and active spirit, and all had a good word for his punctuality.

But William had his trials. One morning he was sent to the bank for money; and returning, laid the pile on the counting room desk. His master was gone, and there was no one in the room but Ashton. Mr. Thomas soon came back.

"Two dollars are missing," said he, counting the money.

The blood mounted to poor William's face, but he answered firmly:—

"I laid it all on your desk, sir."

Mr. Thomas looked steadily into the boy's face,

and seeing nothing but an honest purpose there, said, "Another time put the money into my hands, my boy."

When the busy season came on, one of the head clerks was taken sick, and William rendered him-self useful to the bookkeeper by helping him add some of his tall columns. Oh, how glad he was now for his drilling in arithmetic, as the bookkeeper thanked him for his valuable help.

William Helped the Bookkeeper

Ashton often asked William to go and ride, or to visit the oyster saloons, or the bowling alley, or the theatre. To all invitations of this kind, William had but one answer. He always said he had no time, or money to spare for such things. After the day's work was done, he loved to get back to his chamber to read. He did not crave perpetual excitement, or any more eating and drinking than was supplied at his usual meals.

Not so with Ashton. This young man had indulgent parents, and a plenty of money, or it seemed so to William; and yet he ate it, or drank it, or spent it in other things, as fast and so soon that he was often borrowing from the other clerks.

Ashton joked William upon his "stiff notions," but the truth was that William was far the happier of the two.

At last a half bale of goods was missing; searching inquiries were made, and the theft was traced to Ashton. O the shame and disgrace of the discovery! but alas, it was not his first theft. Ashton had been in the habit of stealing little sums in order to get the means to gratify his taste for pleasure; and now that his guilt had come to light, he ran off, and before his parents were aware of it, fled to a far country, an outcast from his beautiful home, from his afflicted friends, and from all the comforts and blessings of a virtuous life.

William is rapidly rising in the confidence and respect of his employers, fearing God, and faithful in duty.

"An outcast from his beautiful home."

The Fatal Ten Minutes' Delay

"Ten minutes more to sleep in his chair."

TEN MINUTES' DELAY

ALL well-informed people are familiar with the sad account of the death of the young Prince Napoleon, who fell pierced by nineteen wounds at the hands of the Zulus, in South Africa, June 1, 1879.

Many will remember that Capt. Carey, in his published report, mentioned that after they had selected the camping ground,— the object for which the squad of six had been detailed,— and had had coffee and rested, he suggested that they should remount and return to camp. But the young prince, who commanded the squad, said,—

"No, let's wait ten minutes."

Just as they were preparing to remount, at the expiration of that ten minutes, a body of Zulus came on them, and all fled but the prince, whose horse broke from him. After a desperate resistance, he fell, covered with wounds, and died "in the tall grass of the douga."

I presume all do not **know** that this pleading

for ten minutes' delay was a habit of the young prince from early childhood.

A correspondent of a leading Paris journal interviewed the empress as she was about leaving for the scene of the tragedy that had wrecked all her earthly hopes, and drew her into conversation on the subject of her son.

She talked freely during the interview, but with an evident anguish of spirit, which seemed only the more sad from her effort at control.

During this interview, while speaking of the childhood of her son, the prince, she unconsciously revealed the trait in his character that had caused all this woe,— to her, wrecked hopes and a broken heart; to him, the probable loss of a throne, an earthly future, and his life.

After describing her as still lovely in her lonely grief, the writer from whom we quote said :—

" 'The empress had now risen and stood, slightly trembling with emotion, when, stepping rapidly and gracefully across the room, she opened a cabinet, from which she took a pocketbook, and read therefrom on a leaf, 'Going with Carey,'— the last words ever written by the prince; then she added, —'Of all that Captain Carey has ever written in regard to my son, those fatal ten minutes alone, I hold to be true. It was ever his habit,' she continued, 'to plead for ten minutes' delay; so much so that I used to tell him they ought to call him Monsieur Dix Minutes.'

" 'He always begged for ten minutes more sleep

in the morning ; ten minutes more at night to sleep in his chair ; and when too much overcome with sleep to speak, he would hold up his two little hands, the ten fingers representing the ten minutes more for which he pleaded.'"

The habit of procrastination is a deadly foe to all prosperity in temporal or in moral affairs. We ought to do every duty as soon as it can be done.

I HAVE a secret which I should like to whisper to the boys and girls if they will put their ears down close enough. I don't want father and mother to hear — for it is to be a surprise on them.

You have long wanted your own way. You have become tired of hearing mother say, "Come right home after school." "Don't be late." "Be sure to tell the teacher." It is "Do this" and "Don't do that" all the time. You are sick of it, and would like to have your own way. Well, put your ears down while I whisper one word, "Obey."

Oh, you think I am making fun. No, I am not. I know a boy who decided to do just what his father said. He never offered excuses, never tried to get out of work, until finally his father came to trust him perfectly.

His father said, "I know that Harlie will do what is right." When he went out nights, or to school, or to play, his father never said a word, for he had come to have perfect confidence in his boy.

Honestly, obedience is the road to freedom. If you want to have your own way, just begin to obey.

THE PREMIUM

I THINK I am sure of one premium at least," said Edward, as he stood among his schoolfellows.

It was examination day, and many a young heart was beating quick with the hope of approbation and reward, or with the fear of disgrace.

Some had looked forward to this day, and applied to their tasks, knowing how carefully they would be examined, and commended or punished according as they deserved.

Others had chosen to forget that such a day must come, and idled away the time which they would now have given a great deal to have at their disposal again.

In the center of the schoolroom was placed a long table, covered with books of various sizes and of different value. There were Bibles and Testaments, both large and small, the histories of Rome, of Greece, and of England. There were volumes elegantly bound and pamphlets just stitched together.

The school was extensive, and it was desired that every one who had exerted himself to the best of his ability, however little that might be, should carry home with him some mark of encouragement, to remind him that diligence and perseverance were not overlooked.

Like the servants to whom the Lord intrusted the talents, some had five, and some had but one, yet these last could not be excused for hiding and neglecting it because it was small; even the youngest and the simplest child at school may make something of the reason and opportunities which the Lord has given him to improve.

With anxious hearts and earnest faces, the boys arranged themselves around the table; and were examined with great care and patience by their teachers, as to the progress they had made in their studies.

Now, Edward had set his heart on one particular premium, the Roman History, neatly bound, and making two very pretty volumes, which he thought would handsomely fill up a vacant space on his book-shelves.

He allowed himself to think of this until no other prize was of any value in his sight. This is a great fault, often committed by children, and grown people too; instead of thankfully receiving whatever the bounty of Providence assigns them, they would choose for themselves; they become discontented and unhappy in the midst of blessings, because the wisdom of God sees fit to withhold some one thing that their folly deems necessary to their happiness.

Edward passed his examination with much credit, and one of the first premiums was adjudged to him; but instead of the Roman History, a very neat Bible, in excellent large type, was placed in his hands.

Many of his school-mates had longed for that Bible, but Edward did not care for it.

The eyes of the foolish boy filled with tears, as he saw the elegant History of Rome presented to another, who, perhaps would gladly have exchanged with him.

The next day Edward returned home and related

The Teacher Presents the Bible

his disappointment to his parents, who thought his desire for the Roman History a mark of great learning and taste; but since he had distinguished himself so well, they did not much care what prize he received.

Edward's father lived in the country, not far from the seaside, in a most delightful and healthful situation.

At this time his mother's brother, whose health was very poor, came to enjoy the benefit of the sea breezes, and rest a little from the toil and bustle of active life in London.

Mr. Lewis was a young man of the most pleasing manners and appearance. He was gentle and serious, but not at all gloomy or severe.

His bad health only served to increase his patience in enduring it without a murmuring word or discontented look. Edward, who was really a kind-hearted and affectionate boy, soon became very much attached to his uncle, who had not seen him since he was an infant, and who was much pleased at the attentions his nephew delighted to show him.

Young hearts are soon won; and it was only three days after Edward's return from school, that he went bounding over the grounds in search of his uncle, whose society he already preferred to his usual amusements.

Mr. Lewis was seated under a fine old oak, the high and knotted roots of which served as a seat; while the soft moss, in which grew many delicate little flowers, was like a carpet beneath his feet.

A rich and extensive tract of country lay spread before his eyes; and, at a distance the mighty ocean, whose deep green waters were seen in beau-

"Is that a Bible, uncle?"

tiful contrast with the pale yellow cliff, bounded the prospect.

Thin clouds were floating past the sun every now and then, and threw all the varieties of light and shade upon the lovely scene below.

Mr. Lewis had a book in his hand, into which he frequently looked, and then raised his eyes again to gaze upon the beauties of nature that surrounded him.

So intent he seemed that Edward doubted whether he ought to disturb him, until his uncle, seeing him at some little distance, kindly beckoned him to come near.

"Is not this a pretty place, uncle?" asked Edward, as he seated himself beside him; "and do you not find the breeze from the water very refreshing?"

"It is beautiful indeed, my dear boy; and I am refreshed and instructed as I look around me."

The Holy Bible

"Is that a Bible, uncle?"

"Yes. I always find it the best commentary upon His works;—they explain each other."

"I love the Bible too, uncle," said Edward, "and got much credit for my answering on Scripture questions last half-year."

"And which did you enjoy most, Edward, the Scriptures, or the credit you got for studying them?"

Edward looked a little embarrassed and did not immediately reply.

"It is quite right to take pleasure in the well-earned approbation of your teachers," continued Mr. Lewis, "and I was glad to hear that you were given a premium at the last examination also."

"Yes, uncle, but not the prize I wanted most. There was a Roman History that I should have liked better, and it was exactly of equal value with the Bible that I got."

"Of equal value, Edward?"

"I mean that it was not reckoned a higher prize, and it would have been a nicer book for me."

"Then you had a Bible already?"

"Why, no, uncle, not of my own, but it is easy to borrow one on the Sabbath; and I had gone through all my Scripture proofs, and do not want it on other days."

"Read these four verses for me," said Mr. Lewis, pointing to the sixth chapter of Deuteronomy "commencing with the sixth verse."

Edward read: "And these words which I command thee this day, shall be in thine heart; and thou shalt teach them diligently unto thy children, and shalt talk of them when thou sittest in thine house, and when thou walkest by the way, and when thou liest down, and when thou risest up. And thou shalt bind them for a sign upon thine hand, and they shall be as frontlets between thine eyes, and thou shalt write them upon the posts of thy house, and on thy gates."

"To whom did the Lord give this command, Edward?"

"To the Jews, uncle."

"Yes; and the word of God, which cannot pass away, is as much binding on us as on them, in everything excepting the sacrifices and ceremonies, which foreshowed the coming of the Lord Jesus Christ, and which were done away. For by His death He fulfilled all those types and shadows."

"Then," said Edward, "we are commanded to write the Bible on our hands and on our doorposts."

"No, my dear boy, not literally, but in a figure of speech; as the Lord, when declaring he never will forget Zion, says, 'I have graven thee upon the palms of My hands; thy walls are continually before Me.'

"The meaning of the passage you first read is, that we must have the word of God as continually present in our minds as anything written on our hands, and on every object around us, would be to our bodily sight. And how are we to get our thoughts so occupied by it, Edward?"

"By continually reading it I suppose," replied Edward, rather sullenly.

"By reading it often, and meditating on it much," said his uncle; "and that we can do without interfering with our other business. Without prayer, you cannot obtain any spiritual blessing, nor maintain any communion with God; and without reading the Scriptures you will have but little desire to pray.

"We are like people wandering in the dark, while the Bible is as a bright lamp held out to direct us in the only safe path. You cannot be a child of God if you do not His will; you cannot do it unless you know it, and it is by the Bible that He is pleased to have that knowledge known. Do you begin to see, Edward, that the Bible is more suitable as an every-day book than your profane history?"

"Why, yes, uncle; but the Bible is a serious book, and if I read it so constantly, I never should be merry."

"There is no merriment among the lost, Edward;  and that dreadful lot will be your portion if you neglect the great salvation which the Scriptures set forth. Besides, there is no foundation for what you suppose to be the effect of reading the Bible. I have known people naturally melancholy and discontented, become cheerful and happy by studying it; but I never in my life saw an instance of persons becoming unhappy because they had a hope of going to heaven."

"I remember, uncle, that it is written concerning wisdom, that 'her ways are ways of pleasantness, and all her paths are peace.'"

"Most true, my dear boy, 'quietness and assurance forever' is the portion of God's people.

"'Rejoice in the Lord alway, and again I say, rejoice.'

"'The ransomed of the Lord shall return, and come to Zion with songs, and everlasting joy upon their heads; they shall obtain joy and gladness, and sorrow and sighing shall flee away.'

"Are such expressions as these likely to make us gloomy, Edward?"

"O no, uncle; and I often wonder that you, who suffer so much pain, and read the Bible constantly, are not melancholy."

"How can I be melancholy, Edward, when the Bible tells me that all these things are working together for my spiritual good? that He who spared not His own Son, but delivered Him up for us all, will with Him also freely give us all things?

"When I think of what my sins deserve, and see the Lamb of God bearing the chastisement that should fall upon me, how can I be melancholy !

"When I feel that the Spirit of God is bringing these things to my remembrance, and enabling me to love the Lord Jesus, who has done so much for me, must I not rejoice?

"I know that in me, that is, in my flesh, dwelleth no good thing; and since God has promised forgiveness to all who seek that blessing through His Son; and since I feel assured that I have sought that blessing, and feel peace and joy in believing, surely the song of praise, not the moan of lamentation, becomes me.

"Yet I do lament, Edward, daily lament my many offenses against God; but I am assured that Christ's blood cleanseth from all sin, and that in Him I have a powerful and all-prevailing Advocate with the Father. I know in whom I have believed, and that He will never cast off nor forsake me.

"I am sinking into the grave, my dear boy, but I do not shrink from that prospect, because the bitterness of death is taken away by my Saviour, who died for my sins, and rose again for my justification; and though this body returns to dust, I shall live again, and enter into the presence of my Redeemer, and rejoice there evermore."

Edward looked at the animated countenance of his uncle, and then cast down his eyes; they were full of tears. At last he said:—

"Indeed, uncle, I am a very sinful boy, neglecting the Bible, because I know it would show me my sin, and the consequences of it.

"But I will trifle no more with God's displeasure. I will get that precious Bible, worth a thousand Roman histories, and I will read it daily, with prayer, that I may be wise unto salvation."

Mr. Lewis did not live long after this. He died, rejoicing in hope of life eternal; and as often as Edward was allowed to return home from school, he was to be seen under the oak tree, with the Bible in his hand, from which he learned more and more the will of his God and Saviour, the utter sinfulness of his own nature, and his inability to help himself. From this holy word he learned to place all his dependence upon the merits of his Saviour, to follow the example of his Saviour, in prayer, in resignation, and in doing good to the poor.

He often thought of his dear uncle, and counted that day happy when he sat to listen to his kind advice, which brought him to a knowledge of himself and of his heavenly Father.

LESSONS FROM THE 119th PSALM

"Thy word is a lamp unto my feet, and a light unto my path."

"Thou through Thy commandments hast made me wiser than mine enemies."

"I have more understanding than all my teachers: for Thy testimonies are my meditation."

"I understand more than the ancients, because I keep Thy precepts."

"I study two hours before breakfast."

WHERE THE GOLD IS

TOM JONES was a little fellow, and not so quick to learn as some boys; but nobody in the class could beat him in his lessons. He rarely missed in geography, never in spelling, and his arithmetic was always correctly done; as for his reading, no boy improved like him. The boys were fairly angry sometimes, he outdid them so.

"Why, Tom, where do you learn your lessons? You don't study in school more than the other boys."

"I rise early in the morning and study two hours before breakfast," answered Tom.

Ah, that is it! "The morning hour has gold in its mouth."

There is a little garden near us, which is the prettiest and most plentiful little spot in all the neighborhood. The earliest radishes, peas, strawberries, and tomatoes, grow there. It supplies the family with vegetables, besides some for the market.

If anybody wants flowers, that garden is the

place to go for the sweetest roses, pinks and "all sorts," without number. The soil, we used to think, was poor and rocky, besides being exposed to the north wind. The owner is a busy man, yet he never hires.

"How do you make so much out of your little garden?"

"I give my mornings to it," answered the owner, "and I do n't know which is the most benefited by my work, my garden or myself."

Ah, "the morning hour has gold in its month."

———

William Down was one of our young converts. He united with the church, and appeared well; but I pitied the poor fellow when I thought of his going back to the shipyard to work among a gang of godless associates. Will he maintain his stand? I thought. It is so easy to slip back in religion — easier to go back two steps than advance one. Ah, well, we said, we must trust William to his conscience and his Saviour. Two years passed, and instead of William's losing ground, his piety grew brighter and stronger. Others fell away, but not he, and no boy perhaps was placed in more unfavorable circumstances. Talking with William one evening, I discovered one secret of his steadfastness.

"I never, sir, on any account let a single morning pass without secret prayer and the reading of God's word. If I have a good deal to do, I rise an hour earlier. I think over my weak points and try to get God's grace to fortify me just there."

Mark this. Prayer is armor for the battle of life. If you give up your morning petitions, you will suffer for it; temptation is before you, and you are not fit to meet it; there is a guilty feeling in the soul, and you keep at a distance from Christ.

Be sure the hour of prayer broken in upon by sleepiness can never be made up. Make it a principle, young Christian, to begin the day by watching unto prayer. "The morning hour has gold in its mouth;" aye, and something better than gold —heavenly gain.

The Early Morning Reading

"Why do n't you take that fellow in hand."

TAKING HIM IN HAND

TWO boys met in the street and the following conversation ensued : —

"Isaac," said George, "why do n't you take that fellow in hand? he has insulted you almost every day for a week."

"I mean to take him in hand," said Isaac.

"I would make him stop, if I had to take his ears off."

"I mean to make him stop."

"Go and flog him now. I should like to see you do it. You can do it easily enough with one hand."

"I rather think I could; but I'll not try it to-day."

At this point in the conversation the school-boys parted, as they were on their way home, and their roads led them in different directions.

The boy alluded to was the son of an intemperate man, who was angry with Isaac's father, in consequence of some effort to prevent his obtaining rum.

The drunkard's son took up the cause of his

father, and called Isaac hard names every time he
saw him pass; and as he did not do anything by
way of retaliation, he went farther and threw stones
at him.

Isaac was at first provoked at the boy's conduct.
He thought he ought to be thankful that his father
was prevented, in some degree, from procuring
rum, the source of so much misery to himself and
family.

But when he thought of the way in which he
had been brought up, and of the poor lad's ignorance and wretchedness, he pitied him and ceased to
wonder, or to be offended at his conduct.

But Isaac resolved, indeed, to "take him in
hand," and to "stop him," but not in the sense in
which his schoolfellow understood those terms.

The boy's name was James, but he was never
called anything but Jim. Indeed, if you were to
call him by his true name, he would think you
meant somebody else.

The first opportunity Isaac had of "taking him
in hand" was on election day. On that day as
Isaac was on his way home, he saw a group of
boys a little off the road, and heard some shouting
and laughing.

Curiosity led him to the spot. He found that
the boys were gathered around Jim, and another
boy, a good deal larger than he was. This boy was
making fun of Jim's clothes, which were indeed
very ragged and dirty, and telling how he must act
to become as distinguished a man as his father.

Jim was very angry, but when he attempted to strike his persecutor, he would take hold of Jim's hands, and he was so much stronger that he could easily hold them.

Jim then tried kicking, but as he was barefoot, he could not do much execution in that line;

"Isaac remonstrated with the boys."

besides, while he was using one foot in this way, his tormentor would tread upon the other with his heavy boot.

When Isaac came up and saw what was going on, he remonstrated with the boys for countenancing such proceedings; and such was his influence, and the force of truth, that most of them agreed that it was "too bad;" though he was such an "ugly boy," they said, "that he was hardly worth pitying."

The principal actor, however, did not like Isaac's interference; but he soon saw that Isaac was not

afraid of him, and that he was too popular with the
boys to be made the object of abuse. As he turned
to go away, Isaac said to Jim :—

"I'll keep my eyes upon you, and when you go
home, I'll go with you. It is on my way ; they
sha n't hurt you; so do n't cry any more. Come
Jim, go home with me ; I'm going now," continued
Isaac.

Jim did not look up or make any answer. He
did not know what to make of Isaac's behavior
toward him. It could not be because he was afraid
of him, and wished to gain his good will, for Isaac
was not afraid of one much stronger than he. He
had never heard of the command, "Love your
enemies, bless them that curse you, do good to them
that hate you," for he had never been to Sabbath
school, and could not read the Bible.

He followed silently and sullenly, pretty near to
Isaac, till he had reached home, if that sacred name
can with propriety be applied to such a wretched
abode of sin and misery.

He parted from Isaac without thanking him for
his good offices in his behalf. This Isaac did not
wonder at, considering the influences under which
the poor lad had grown up. That he parted with
him without abusing him, Isaac considered as
something gained.

The next morning George and Isaac met on their
way to school. As they passed the drunkard's
dwelling, Jim was at the door, but he did not look
up or say anything as they passed. He looked very

much as though he had been whipped. George did not know what had taken place the day before.

"What keeps Jim so still?" said he.

"Oh, I've had him in hand."

"Jim was at the door, but he did not look up or say anything."

"Have you! I'm glad of it. When was it?"

"Yesterday."

"At election?"

"Yes."

"Anybody see you do it?"

"Yes; some of the boys."

"Found it easy enough, didn't you?"

"Yes."

"Did you give him enough to stop him?"

"I guess so; he is pretty still this morning, you see."

Upon the strength of this conversation, George circulated a report that Isaac had flogged Jim. This created a good deal of surprise, as it was not

in keeping with Isaac's character. The report at
length reached the ears of the teacher.

He inquired about the matter, of Isaac, and

learned that George had
been deceived, or rather had
deceived himself. He
warmly commended Isaac
for his new mode of taking
his enemies "in hand," and
advised him to continue to
practice it. A few days
afterward, as Isaac was on
his way to school, he met
Jim driving some cattle to
a distant field. The cattle
were very unruly, and Jim

"The cattle were very unruly."

made little headway with them. First one would
run back, and then another, till he began to despair
of being able to drive them to pasture.

He burst out crying, and said, "Oh dear, I can't make them go, and father will kill me if I don't."

Isaac pitied his distress, and volunteered to assist him. It cost him a good deal of running, and kept him from school nearly all the morning. But when the cattle were safe in the pasture, Jim said, "I sha n't stone you any more."

When Isaac reached the schoolhouse he showed signs of the violent exercise he had been taking.

"What has Isaac been about?" was the whispered question which went round. When put to him he replied, "I have been chasing cattle to pasture." He was understood to mean his father's cattle.

After school, he waited till all the pupils had left the schoolroom, before he went up to the teacher to give his excuse for being late at school.

"What made you so late?" asked the teacher.

"I was taking Jim in hand again, sir;" and he gave him an account of his proceeding, adding at the close, "I thought you would excuse me, sir."

"Very well, you are excused."

Reader, if you have enemies who annoy you, *take them in hand* in the same way that Isaac did, and you will be certain, if you persevere to conquer them.

Learning the Printer's Trade

OVERWORKED BOYS

THE boys of our time are too much afraid of work. They act as if the honest sweat of the brow was something to be ashamed of. Would that they were all equally afraid of a staggering gait and bloated face! This spirit of laziness builds the gambling houses, fills the jails, supplies the saloons and gaming places with loiterers, and keeps the alms houses and charitable institutions doing a brisk business.

It does n't build mammoth stores and factories, nor buildings like the Astor Library and Cooper Institute. The men who built such monuments of their industry and benevolence were not afraid of work.

All the boys have heard of the great publishing house of the Harpers. They know of their finely illustrated papers and books of all kinds, and perhaps have seen their great publishing house in New York City. But if I should ask the boys how the eldest of the brothers came to found such an illustrious house, I should perhaps be told that he was a "wonderfully lucky man."

He was lucky, and an old friend and fellow-workman, a leading editor, has revealed the secret of his luck. He and the elder Harper learned their trade together, many years ago, in John Street, New York. They began life with no fortune but

"Let's break the back of another token."

willing hands and active brains;—fortune enough for any young man in this free country.

"Sometimes after we had done a good day's work, James Harper would say, 'Thurlow, let's break the back of another *token* (a quarter of a ream of paper),—just break its back.' I would generally reluctantly consent just to *break the back* of the *token;* but James would beguile me, or laugh at my complaints, and never let me off until the *token* was *completed*, fair and square!

"It was our custom in summer to do a fair half-day's work before the other boys and men got their breakfast. We would meet by appointment in the gray of the morning, and go down to John Street. We got the key of the office by tapping on the window, and Mr. Seymour would take it from under his pillow, and hand it to one of us through the blind.

"It kept us out of mischief, and put money into our pockets."

The key handed through the window tells the secret of the *luck* that enabled these two men to rise to eminence, while so many boys that lay soundly sleeping in those busy morning hours are unknown.

No wonder that James Harper became mayor of the city, and head of one of the largest publishing houses in the world. When his great printing house burned down, the giant perseverance which he had learned in those hours of *overwork*, made him able to·raise, from the ashes, a larger and finer one.

Instead of watching till his employer's back was turned, and saying, "Come, boys, let's go home; we've done enough for one day," and sauntering off with a cigar in his mouth, his cry was, "Let's do a little *overwork*."

That *overwork* which frightens boys nowadays out of good places, and sends them out West, on shipboard, anywhere, eating husks, in search of a spot where money can be had without work, laid the foundation of the apprentice boy's future greatness.

Such busy boys were only too glad to go to bed and sleep soundly. They had no time nor spare strength for dissipation, and idle thoughts, and vulgar conversation.

Almost the last words that James Harper uttered were appropriate to the end of such a life, and ought to be engraven upon the mind of every boy who expects to make anything of himself: "*It is not best to be studying how little we can work, but how much.*"

Boys, make up your minds to one thing,—the future great men of this country are doing just what those boys did. If you are dodging work, angry at your employer or teacher for trying to make you faithful; if you are getting up late, cross, and sleepy, after a night of pleasure-seeking, longing for the time when you can exchange honest work for speculation, you will be a victim to your own folly.

It is not best to study how little we can work, but how much

The plainly-dressed boys whom you meet carrying packages, going of errands, working at trades, following the plow, are laying up stores of what you call *good luck*. Overwork has no terrors for them. They are preparing to take the places of the great leaders of our country's affairs. They have learned James Harper's *secret*. The key handed out to him in the "gray of the morning" —*that* tells the story!

> "The heights by great men reached and kept
>   Were not attained by sudden flight
> But they, while their companions slept,
>   Were toiling upward in the night."

Bring Your Wood Saws and Axes

THE BEST FUN

NOW, boys, I'll tell you how we can have some fun," said Fred Blake to his companions, who had assembled on a beautiful, moonlight evening for sliding, snowballing, and fun generally.

"How?" "Where?" "What is it?" asked several eager voices together.

"I heard Widow More tell a man a little while ago," replied Fred, "that she would go to sit up with a sick child to-night. She said she would be there about eight o'clock. Now, as soon as she is gone, let's make a big snow man on her doorstep so that when she comes home, she cannot get in without first knocking him down."

"Capital!" shouted several of the boys.

"See here," said Charlie Neal, "I'll tell you the best fun."

"What is it?" again inquired several at once.

"Wait awhile," said Charlie. "Who has a wood-saw?"

"I have," "So have I," answered three of the

"We can saw and split this pile of wood."

boys. "But what in the world do you want a
wood saw for?"

"You shall see," replied Charlie. "It is almost
eight o'clock now, so go and get your saws. You,
Fred and Nathan, get each an axe, and I will get a
shovel. Let us all be back here in fifteen minutes,
and then I'll show you the fun."

The boys separated to go on their several
errands, each wondering what the fun could be,
and what possible use could be made of wood saws
and axes, in their play. But Charlie was not only
a great favorite with them all, but also an ac-
knowledged leader, and they fully believed in him
and his promise.

Anxious to know what the "fun" was which
Charlie had for them, they made haste, and were
soon on hand, with their saws, axes, and shovels.

"Now," said Charlie, "Mrs. More is gone, for I
met her when I was coming back; so let's be off at
once."

"But what are you going to do?" inquired
several impatient members of the party.

"You shall see directly," replied the leader, as
they approached the humble home of Mrs. More.

"Now, boys," said Charlie, "you see that pile of
wood; a man hauled it here this afternoon, and I
heard Mrs. More tell him that unless she got some
one to saw it to-night, she would have nothing to
make a fire with in the morning. Now, we can saw
and split that pile of wood just about as easy as we
could build a great snow man, and when Mrs.

More comes home from her watching, she will be
fully as much surprised to find her wood sawed, as
she would to find a snow man at her doorstep, and
a great deal more pleasantly, too. What say you
—will you do it?

One or two of the boys
demurred at first, but the
majority were in favor of
Charley's project; so all
finally joined in, and went
to work with a will.

"I'll go round to the
back of the shed," said
Charley, "and crawl
through the window and
unfasten the door. Then
we'll take turns in sawing,
splitting, and carrying in
the wood; and I want to
pile it up nicely, and to
shovel all the snow away
from the door; and make
a good wide path, too, from
the door to the street:
What fun it will be when
she comes home and sees it?"

Carrying in the Wood

The boys began to appreciate the fun, for they
felt that they were doing a good deed, and experi-
enced the satisfaction which always results from
well-doing.

It was not a long, wearisome job, for seven robust and healthy boys to saw, split, and pile up the poor widow's half-cord of wood, and to shovel a good path.

When it was done, so great was their pleasure, that one of the boys, who objected to the work at first, proposed that they should go to a neighboring carpenter's shop, where plenty of shavings could be had for the carrying away, and each bring an armful of kindling wood. This they did, and afterward hurried home, all of them more than satisfied with the "fun" of the winter evening.

The next morning, when Mrs. More came home, weary from watching by the sick bed, and saw what was done, she was very much surprised. When she was told who had done it, by a neighbor, who had witnessed the kindly deed, her fervent prayer, "God bless the boys!" was, of itself, an abundant reward for their labors.

Boys and girls, the best fun is always found in doing something that is kind and useful. If you doubt it in the least, just try it for yourselves, and you will be convinced.

"I'll help you across, if you wish to go."

SOMEBODY'S MOTHER

THE woman was old, and ragged and gray,
And bent with the chill of a winter's day;

The street was wet with recent snow,
And the woman's feet were aged and slow,

She stood at the crossing, and waited long,
Alone, uncared for amid the throng

Of human beings who passed her by,
Nor heeded the glance of her anxious eye.

Down the street with laugh and shout,
Glad in the freedom of "school is out,"

Came the boys like a flock of sheep,
Hailing the snow piled white and deep.

Past the woman so old and gray
Hastened the children on their way,

Nor offered a helping hand to her,
So meek, so timid, afraid to stir

[188]

Lest the carriage wheels or the horses' feet
Should crowd her down in the slippery street.

At last came out of the merry troop
The gayest laddie of all the group;

He paused beside her, and whispered low,
"I'll help you across, if you wish to go."

Her aged hand on his strong young arm
She placed, and so, without hurt or harm,

He guided the trembling feet along,
Proud that his own were firm and strong.

Then back again to his friends he went,
His young heart happy and well content.

"She's somebody's mother, boys, you know,
For all that she's aged and poor and slow;

"And I hope some fellow will lend a hand
To help *my* mother, you understand,

"If ever she's poor and old and gray,
When her own dear boy is far away."

And "somebody's mother" bowed low her head
In her home that night, and the prayer she said

Was, "God be kind to the noble boy,
Who is somebody's son and pride and joy!"

The Grist Mill

WAITING FOR THE GRIST

IT is impossible to measure the influence which may be exerted by a single act, a word, or even a look. It was the simple act of an entire stranger that changed the course of my whole life.

When I was a boy, my father moved to the Far West—Ohio. It was before the days of steam, and no great mills thundered on her river banks, but occasionally there was a little gristmill by the side of some small stream.

To these little mills, the surrounding neighborhood flocked with their sacks of corn. Sometimes we had to wait two or three days for our turn. I was generally the one sent from our house, for, while I was too small to be of much account on the farm, I was as good as a man to carry a grist to mill. So I was not at all surprised one morning when my father said, "Henry, you must take the horse and go to mill to-day."

But I found so many of the neighboring farmers there ahead of me, that I knew there was no hope of getting home that day; but I was not at all sorry, for my basket was well filled with provisions, and Mr. Saunders always opened his big barn for us to sleep in.

That day there was an addition to the number who had been in the habit of gathering, from time to time, in the old Saunders barn,—a young fellow about my own age. His name was Charley Allen, and his father had bought a farm over on the Brush Creek road. He was sociable and friendly, but somehow I felt that he had "more manners" than the rest of us.

The evening was spent, as usual, in relating coarse jokes and playing cards. Although I was not accustomed to such things at home, I had become so used to it at the mill, that it had long since ceased to shock me, and, indeed, I was getting to enjoy watching the games of the others.

When bedtime came, we were all so busy with our own affairs that we did not notice Charley Allen, until a rude, profane fellow exclaimed : —

"Heyday! we've got a parson here!" sure enough. Charley was kneeling by the oatbin praying. But the jest met with no response. The silence was broken only by the drowsy cattle below, and the twittering swallows overhead. More than one rough man wiped a tear from his eyes as he went silently to his bed on the hay.

I had always been in the habit of praying at home, but I never thought of such a thing at Saunder's Mill.

As I laid awake that night in the old barn, think-

ing of Charley Allen's courage, and what an effect
it had upon the men, I firmly resolved that in the
future I would *do right*.   I little thought how soon
my courage would be tested.

Just after dinner I got my grist, and started for
home.   When I arrived at Squire Albright's gate,
where I turned off to go home, I found the old
squire waiting for me.   I saw in a moment that

"Did you go through this gate yesterday?"

something had gone wrong.   I had always stood in
the greatest awe of the old gentlemen, because he
was the rich man of the neighborhood, and, now
I felt my heart beginning to beat very fast.   As
soon as I came near he said:—

"Did you go through this gate yesterday?"

I could easily have denied it, as it was before
daylight when I went through, and I quite as often

went the other way. But the picture of Charley Allen kneeling in the barn, came to my mind like a flash, and before I had time to listen to the tempter I replied : —

"Yes, sir ; I did."

"Are you sure you shut and pinned the gate?" he asked.

This question staggered me. I remembered distinctly that I did not. I could pull the pin out without getting off my horse, but I could not put it in again ; so I carelessly rode away, and left it open.

"I—I—I—"

"Out with it; tell just what you did!"

"I left it open," I said abruptly.

"Well, you let the cattle in and they have destroyed all my early potatoes,—a terrible piece of business!"

"I'm very sorry, I'd—"

"Talking won't help matters now ; but remember, boy, remember that sorrow doesn't make potatoes,—sorrow doesn't make potatoes."

I felt very bad about the matter, for I was really sorry that the old gentleman had lost his potatoes, and then I expected to be severely reproved at home. But I soon found that they knew nothing of the matter, and after several days had passed, I began to rest quite easy.

Alas for human hopes! one rainy afternoon I saw the squire riding down the lane. I ran off to the barn, ashamed to face him, and afraid to meet my father.   They sat on the porch and talked for a long time.

At last my curiosity overcame my fear, and I stole back to the house, and went into mother's room to see if I could hear what they were talking about.

"Why. the boy could be spared well enough, but he does n't know anything about the business," said my father.

"There is one thing he does know," said the squire, "he knows how to tell the truth."   He then related the circumstance which I so much dreaded to have my father hear.

After he had gone, my father called me to him, and told me that the squire was going to start a store in the village, and wanted a boy to help, and that I could go if I wished.   I went, and remained in the village store until it became a city store.   People say that I got my start in life when I entered Albright's store, but I will always declare that I got it while I was waiting for the grist.

"Twenty dollars against themselves."

A BOY'S LESSONS IN DISHONESTY

HAVE you examined that bill, James?"

"Yes, sir."

"Anything wrong?"

"I find two errors."

"Ah, let me see."

The lad handed his employer a long bill that had been placed on his desk for examination.

"Here is an error of ten dollars in the calculation which they have made against themselves; and another of ten dollars in the footing."

"Also against themselves?"

"Yes, sir."

The merchant smiled in a way that struck the lad as peculiar.

"Twenty dollars against themselves," he remarked in a kind of pleased surprise; "trusty clerks they must have!"

"Shall I correct the figures?" asked the lad.

"No; let them correct their own mistakes. We don't examine bill's for other people's benefit,"

replied the merchant. "It will be time to correct
those errors when they find them out. All so
much gain as it now stands."

The boy's delicate moral sense was shocked at so
unexpected a remark. He was the son of a poor
widow, who had taught him that to be just is the
duty of man, and that "honesty is the best policy"
always.

Mr. Carman, the merchant, in whose employment the lad James had been for only a few
months, was an old friend of James's father, and a
man in whom he had the highest confidence. In
fact, James had always looked upon him as a kind
of model man. When Mr. Carman agreed to take
him into his store, the lad felt that great good fortune was in his way.

"Let them correct their own mistakes." These
words made a strong impression on the mind of
James Lewis. When first spoken by Mr. Carman,
with the meaning which he gave them, as we have
said, he felt shocked. But as he turned them over
again in his thoughts, and remembered that this
man stood very high in his mother's estimation, he
began to think that perhaps the thing was fair
enough in business. Mr. Carman was hardly the
man to do wrong.

A few days after James had examined the bill, a
clerk from the house which had sent it, called for
settlement. The lad, who was present, waited with
interest to see whether Mr. Carman would speak of
the error. But he made no remark. A check for

the amount of the bill as rendered, was filled up, and a receipt taken.

"Is that right?" James asked himself this question. His conscience said no. The fact that Mr. Carman had so acted, bewildered his mind.

"It may be the way in business"—he thought to himself—"but it does n't look honest. I would n't have believed it of him."

Mr. Carman had a way with him that won the boy's heart, and naturally tended to make him judge of whatever he might do in a most favorable manner.

"I wish he had corrected that error," he said to himself a great many times when congratulating himself upon his own good fortune in having been received into Mr. Carman's employment. "It does n't look right, but it *may* be in the way of business."

One day he went to the bank and drew the money for a check. In counting it over, he found that the teller had paid him fifty dollars too much. So he went back to the counter and told him of his mistake. The teller thanked him, and he returned to the store with the consciousness in his mind of having done right.

"The teller overpaid me fifty dollars," he said to Mr. Carman, as he handed him the money.

"Indeed," replied the latter, a light breaking over his countenance; and he hastily counted the bank bills.

The light faded as the last bill left his fingers.

"There's no mistake, James." A tone of disappointment was in his voice.

"Oh, I gave them back the fifty dollars. Wasn't that right?"

"You simpleton!" exclaimed Mr. Carman. "Don't you know that bank mistakes are never corrected? If the teller had paid you fifty dollars short he would not have made it right."

The warm blood mantled the cheek of James under this reproof. It is often the

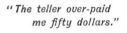

"The teller over-paid me fifty dollars."

"You simpleton."

case that more shame is felt for a blunder than for a crime. In this instance the lad felt a sort of mortification at having done what Mr. Carman was pleased to call a silly thing, and he made up his mind that if they should ever over-pay him a thousand dollars at the bank, he should bring the amount to his employer, and let him do as he pleased with the money.

"Let people look out for their own mistakes," said Mr. Carman.

James Lewis pondered these things in his heart. The impression they made was too strong ever to be forgotten. "It may be right," he said, but he did not feel altogether satisfied.

A month or two after this last occurrence, as James counted over his weekly wages, just received from Mr. Carman, he saw that he had been paid a half dollar too much.

His first impulse was to return the half dollar to his employer, and it was on his lips to say, "You have given me a half dollar too much, sir," when the unforgotten words, "Let people look after their own mistakes," flashing into his mind, made him hesitate. To parley with evil is to be overcome.

"I must think about this," said James, as he put the

"He had been paid a half dollar too much."

money into his pocket. "If it is right in one case, it is right in another. Mr. Carman doesn't correct mistakes that people make in his favor, and he can't complain when the rule works against himself."

But the boy was very far from being comfortable. He felt that to keep a half dollar would be a dishonest act. Still he could not make up his mind to return it, at least not then.

James did not return the half-dollar, but spent it for his gratification. After he had done this, it came suddenly into his head that Mr. Carman had only been trying him, and he was filled with anxiety and alarm.

Not long after this Mr. Carman repeated the same mistake. Again James kept the half-dollar, and with less hesitation.

"Let him correct his own mistakes," said he resolutely; "that's the doctrine he acts upon with other people, and he can't complain if he gets paid in the same coin he puts in circulation. I just wanted a half dollar."

From this time, the fine moral sense of James Lewis was blunted and his conscience troubled him but little. He began to cherish a spirit of covetousness, which is in the heart of all, until subdued by the grace of Christ. He soon began to desire the possession of things for which he was not able to pay.

James had good business qualifications. This pleased Mr. Carman. He saw that the young man was intelligent, industrious, and tactful with customers. For this reason, he advanced him rapidly, and, before he was eighteen years of age, he held the most responsible position in the store.

But James had learned something more from his

employer than the secret of doing business well. He had learned to be dishonest. He had never forgotten the first lesson he had received in the downward course. And this wicked instruction he had acted upon, not only in two instances, but in a hundred, and almost always to the injury of Mr. Carman.

The young man had long since given up waiting for mistakes to be made in his favor. He originated them in the varied and complicated transactions of a large business in which he was trusted implicity.

Of course, he grew to be sharp and cunning; always on the alert; always bright, and ready skillfully to meet any approaches towards a discovery of his wrong-doing by his employer, who held him in high regard.

In this way it went on until James Lewis was in his twentieth year. Then the merchant received a letter which aroused his suspicions. This letter spoke of the young man as not keeping the most respectable company, and as spending money too freely for a clerk on a moderate salary.

Before this time James and his mother had removed into a pleasant house, for which he paid a rent of four hundred dollars yearly. His salary was only eight hundred dollars, but he deceived his mother by telling her that it was fifteen hundred. Every comfort that she needed was fully supplied, and she was beginning to feel that, after a long struggle with the world, her happier days had come.

James was at his desk when the letter was received by Mr. Carman. He looked at his employer,
and saw him change countenance suddenly. The
letter was read twice, and James saw that the contents appeared to disturb his
employer. Mr. Carman glanced
toward the desk and their eyes

"The look that James received made his heart stop beating."

met. It was only for a moment, but the look that
James received made his heart stop beating.

There was something about the movements of
the merchant for the rest of the day that troubled
the young man. It was plain to him that suspi-
cion had been aroused by that letter. Oh, how bit-
terly now did he repent! How he dreaded discovery
and punishment! Exposure would disgrace and
ruin him, and bow the head of his widowed mother
even to the grave.

That evening at supper, Mrs. Lewis noticed that
her son did not eat; and that his face was troubled.

"You are not well," she said "perhaps a rest will make you feel better."

"It's nothing but a headache; I'll lie down on the sofa in the parlor a little while."

Mrs. Lewis followed him into the parlor shortly, and sitting down on the sofa on which he was lying, placed her hand upon his head. Ah, it would take more than the loving pressure of a mother's hand to ease the pain which he was suffering. The touch of that pure hand increased the pain to agony.

"Do you feel better?" asked Mrs. Lewis. She had remained some time with her hand on his forehead.

"Not much," he replied; "I think a walk in the open air will do me good," he added, rising.

"Don't go out, James," said Mrs. Lewis, a troubled feeling coming into her heart.

"I'll only walk a few squares," he replied, as he hurried down the street.

"There is something more than headache the matter with him," thought Mrs. Lewis.

For half an hour James walked without any purpose in his mind beyond the escape from the presence of his mother. At last his walk brought him near Mr. Carman's store, and in passing, he was surprised at seeing a light within.

"What can this mean?" he asked himself, a new fear creeping into his trembling heart.

He listened by the door and windows, but he could hear no sound within.

"There's something wrong," he said; "what can it be? If this is discovered what will be the end of it? Ruin! ruin! O my poor mother!"

The wretched young man hastened on, walking the streets for two hours, when he returned home. His mother met him when he entered, and with unconcealed anxiety, asked him if he were better. He said "yes," but in a manner that only increased the trouble she felt. He then passed hastily to his own room.

In the morning the strangely altered face of her son as he met his mother at the breakfast table, struck alarm to her heart. He was silent, and evaded all her questions. While they still sat at the table, the door bell rang loudly. The sound startled James, and he turned his head nervously to listen.

"Who is it?" asked Mrs. Lewis.

"A gentleman who wishes to see Mr. James," replied the girl.

James rose instantly and went out into the hall, shutting the dining-room door as he did so. Mrs. Lewis sat waiting her son's return. She heard him coming back in a few moments; but he did not enter the dining-room. Then he returned along the hall to the street door, and she heard it shut. All was silent. Starting up, she ran into the passage, but James was not there. He had gone away with the person who called.

Ah, that was a sad home leaving. Mr. Carman had spent half the night in examining the accounts that had been kept by James. He discovered frauds of over six thousand dollars. Blindly indignant, he had sent an officer to arrest him early in the morning. It was with this officer that he went away from his mother, *never to return.*

"The young villain shall lie in the bed he has made for himself!" exclaimed Mr. Carman, in his bitter indignation. And he made a complete exposure. At the trial he showed an eager desire to have him convicted, and presented such an array of evidence that the jury could not give any other verdict than guilty.

The poor mother was in court, and sobbed as she heard

The Arrest of James

the evidences of the guilt of her son. The presiding judge addressed the culprit, and asked if he had anything to say why sentence should not be pronounced against him. The prisoner arose, and said:

"I went into that man's store an innocent boy."

"Will it please your honor to ask my prosecutor to come a little nearer, so that I can look at him and your honor at the same time?"

Mr. Carman was directed to come forward. James looked at him a few moments, and turned to the judge.

"What I have to say to your honor is this" (he spoke calmly and distinctly), "and it may, in a degree, excuse, though it cannot justify, my crime. I went into that man's store an innocent boy. If he had been an honest man, I would not stand before you to-day as a criminal!"

Mr. Carman appealed to the court for protection against that which he called an outrageous attack upon his character; but he was ordered to be silent. James went on in a firm voice : —

"Only a few weeks after I began work in this man's store, I examined a bill, by his direction, and discovered an error of twenty dollars."

The face of Mr. Carman was crimson.

"You remember it, I see," said James, "and I shall have cause to remember it as long as I live. I asked if I should correct the figures, and you answered : —

"'No; let them correct their own mistakes. We don't examine bills for other people's benefit.'

"It was my first lesson in dishonesty. I saw the bill settled, and Mr. Carman took twenty dollars that was not his own. I felt shocked at first. It seemed such a wrong thing. But soon after this, he called me a simpleton for handing back a fifty-dollar bill to the teller of a bank, which he had overpaid me on a check, and then "—

"May I ask the protection of the court?" said Mr. Carman.

"Is the story of the lad true?" asked the judge.

Mr. Carman looked confused. All felt certain that he was guilty of leading the unhappy young man astray.

"Not long afterward," resumed the young man, "in receiving my wages, I found that Mr. Carman had paid me fifty cents too much. I was about to give it back to him, when I remembered his remark about letting people correct their own mistakes, and I said to myself, 'let him discover and correct his own errors.' Then I dishonestly kept the money.

"Again the same thing happened, and again I kept the money that did not belong to me. This was the beginning of evil, and here I am. If he had shown any mercy to me, I might have kept silent and made no defense."

The young man covered his face with his hands, and sat down overpowered with his feelings. His mother who was near him, sobbed aloud, and bending over, laid her hands on his head. "My poor boy! my poor boy!" she murmured.

There were few undimmed eyes in the court-room. In the silence that followed, Mr. Carman exclaimed : —

"Is my character to be thus blasted on the word of a criminal, your honor? Is this right?"

"Your solemn oath that this charge is untrue,"

said the judge, "will clear your reputation in the eyes of the people."

At these words, James Lewis stood up again instantly. It was the unhappy boy's only opportunity, and the court felt bound in humanity to hear

"Let him take his oath if he dare!"

him. Turning his eyes upon Mr. Carman, he exclaimed : —

"Let him take his oath if he dare!"

Mr. Carman consulted with his counsel, and withdrew.

The judge then arose to pass sentence.

"In consideration of your youth, and the temptation to which in tender years you were subjected,
the court gives you the lightest sentence,—one
year's imprisonment. But let me solemnly warn
you against any further steps in the way you have
taken. Crime can have no valid excuse. It is evil
in the sight of God and man, and leads only to suffering. When you come forth again after your imprisonment, may it be with the resolution to die
rather than commit crime!"

A year afterward, when James Lewis came from
prison, his mother was dead. From the day her
pale face faded from his vision as he passed from
the court-room, he never saw her again.

Ten years thereafter a man was reading a newspaper in a far Western town. He had a calm,
serious face, and looked like one who had known
suffering and trial.

"Brought to justice at last!" he said to himself,
with deep emotion. "Convicted on the charge of
open insolvency, and sent to state prison. So much
for the man who gave me in tender years the first
lessons in wrong-doing. But thank God! another
lesson,—the words of the judge, spoken to me so
many years ago,—have been remembered. 'When
you come forth again, may it be with the resolution to die rather than commit crime!' and I have
kept these words in my heart when there seemed
no way of escaping except through crime. And
God helping me, I will remember them as long as
I live."

" Is your boy sick ?   He was not in school to-day."

"A PICTURE OF GOD."

IT is fairly pathetic what a stranger God is in His own world. He comes to His own, and they who are His own kinsfolk keep Him standing outside the door while they peer suspiciously at Him through the crack at the hinges.

To know God really, truly, is the beginning of a normal life. One of the best pictures of God that I ever saw came to me in a simple story. It was of a man, a minister, who lived in a New England town, who had a son, about fourteen years of age, going to school. One afternoon the boy's teacher called at the home, and asked for the father, and said : —

"Is your boy sick?"

"No. Why?"

" He was not at school to-day."

"Is that so?"

"Nor yesterday."

"You don't mean it!"

"Nor the day before."

"Well!"

"And I supposed he was sick."

"No, he's not sick."

"Well, I thought I should tell you."

And the father said, "Thank you," and the teacher left.

And the father sat thinking. By and by he heard a click at the gate, and he knew the boy was coming, so he went to open the door. And the boy knew as he looked up that his father knew about those three days. And the father said:—

"Come into the library, Phil." And Phil went, and the door was shut. And the father said: "Phil, your teacher was here this afternoon. He tells me you were not at school to-day, nor yesterday nor the day before. And we supposed you were. You let us think you were. And you do not know how badly I feel. I have always trusted you. I have always said, 'I can trust my boy Phil.' And here you've been a living lie for three whole days. And I can't tell you how badly I feel about it."

Well, that was hard on Phil to be talked to quietly like that. If his father had spoken to him roughly, or—had asked him out to the woodshed for a confidential interview, it would not have been nearly so hard. Then, after a moment's pause, the father said, "Phil, we'll get down and pray." And the thing was getting harder for Phil all the time.

He did n't want to pray just then. And they got down. And the father poured out his heart in prayer. And the boy knew as he listened how badly his father felt over his conduct. Somehow he saw himself in the mirror on his knees as he had not before. It's queer about that mirror of the knee-joints. It does show so many things. Many folks do n't like it.

And they got up. And the father's eyes were wet. And Phil's eyes were not dry. Then the father said : —

" My boy, there's a law of life that where there is sin, there is suffering. You can't detach those two things. Where there is suffering there has been sin somewhere. And where there is sin there will be suffering. You can't get these two things apart. Now," he went on, "you have done wrong. And I am in this home like God is in the world. So we will do this. You go up to the attic. I'll make a pallet for you there. We'll take your meals up to you at the regular times, and you stay up there as long as you've been a living lie — three days and three nights."

And Phil did n't say a word. They went up stairs, the pallet was made, and the father kissed his boy and left him alone with his thoughts. Supper time came, and the father and mother sat down to eat. But they could n't eat for thinking about the boy. The longer they chewed upon the food, the bigger and dryer it got in their mouths. And swallowing it was clear out of the question. Then

they went into the sitting room for the evening.
He picked up the evening paper to read, and she
sat down to sew.   Well, his eyes weren't very good.
He wore glasses.   And this evening he could n't
seem to see distinctly — the glasses seemed blurred.
It must have been the glasses, of course.   So he
took them off and cleaned them very deliberately
and then found that he had been holding the paper
upside down.   And she tried to sew.   But the
thread broke, and she could n't seem to get the
needle threaded again.   You could see they were
both bothered.   How we do reveal ourselves in the
details !

By and by the clock struck nine, and then ten,
their usual hour for retiring.   But they made no
move toward retiring.   She said, " Are n't you going
to bed? "   And he said, "I think I'll not go yet a
bit ; you go."   " No, I guess I'll wait a while, too."
And the clock struck eleven, and the hands worked
around toward twelve.   Then they arose, and
locked up, and went to bed, but — not to sleep.
Each one made pretence to be asleep, and each one
knew the other was not asleep.   By and by she
said (women are always the keener), "Why do n't
you sleep? "   And he said gently, " How did you
know I was n't sleeping?   Why do n't you sleep? "

" Well, I just can't for thinking of the boy up in
the attic."

"That's the bother with me," he replied.   And
the clock in the hall struck twelve, and one, and
two.   Still no sleep came.

At last he said, "Mother, I can't stand this any longer; I'm going up stairs with Phil." And he took his pillow and went softly out of the room, and up the attic stairs, and pressed the latch-key softly, so as not to wake the boy if he were asleep, and tiptoed across the attic floor to the corner by the window, and looked — there Phil lay, wide awake, with something glistening in his eyes, and what looked like stains on his cheeks. And the father got down in between the sheets with his boy, and they got their arms around each other's necks, for they had always been the best of friends, father and boy, and their tears got mixed up on each other's cheeks. Then they slept.

"I'm going up stairs with Phil."

And the next night when the time came for sleep, the father said, "Good-night, mother, I'm going up stairs with Phil." And the second night he slept in the attic with his boy. And the third night, again he said, "Mother, good-night, I'm going up with the boy again." And the third night he slept in the place of punishment with his son.

You are not surprised to know that to-day that boy, a man grown, is telling the story of Jesus with tongue and life of flame in the heart of China.

Do you know, I think that father is the best picture of God I ever saw. God could not take away sin. It's here. He could not take away suffering out of kindness to man. For suffering is sin's index finger, saying, "There's something wrong here." So He came down in the person of His Son, and lay down alongside of man for three days and three nights. That's God — our God. And beyond that He comes and puts His life alongside of yours and mine, and makes us hate the bad, and long to be pure. To be on intimate terms with Him, to live in the atmosphere of His presence, to spend the day with Him — that is the true normal life.

Jack and David Jamison going to Mill

IF YOU ARE ONLY HONEST

IT is not best to try to still the voice of conscience by repeating the popular maxim, "If you are only honest, that is all."

The mill was doing a great business that day, when Jack and David Jamison rode up with their bag of corn to be ground. They lived on a small farm five miles off the main road, and were not sorry at the prospect of waiting several hours for their grist.

This would give them a chance of seeing something of the liveliness and bustle of "The Corner," as that part of the village was called, where stood the tavern, the store, and the mill.

Jack and David had plenty of time, and they ran about a great deal, here and there, and saw and heard many things.

At last, a heavy shower coming on, they went back to the mill to eat their lunch, and to inquire when their turn would come.

There they found the miller's son and the son of
the squire engaged in earnest conversation, which
soon took Jack's attention. The miller's son was
urging upon the squire's son the importance of
a correct understanding of the Bible. But the
squire's son only insisted that "*It does n't matter
what a man believes, if he is only sincere.*"

Jack was a vain, foolish fellow, and felt very
much pleased with the rattling off-hand speech of
the squire's son, and he only wished that *he* could
talk as well; then he would put his old grandfather
to confusion — indeed he would.

"*It is no matter what a man believes, provided
he is sincere,*" muttered Jack, bracing his conscience against the godly conversation of his rela-
tives; "I'll fix 'em now," he said to himself, with
a decided nod of the head.

Late in the afternoon the boys' grist was ready;
then the old horse was brought out of the shed, the
bag of meal placed across her back, and Jack and
David both mounted; boys, horse, and bag, all
homeward bound.

"You have a longer ride ahead than I wish you
had, boys," said the miller, casting his eyes toward
a dark cloud which was rising and darkening the
western sky; "there's plenty of water up there for
my mill."

But they set off briskly, and were soon lost to
sight among the windings of the forest road. But
the gloom gathered faster than the horse trotted, so
that it was quite dark when they reached a fork in

the road where it might make considerable difference which road they took.   One was the main
road; this way there was a good bridge over
Bounding Brook, a mountain stream which was
often dangerously swollen by the spring rains.   It
was the safest, though the longest way home.

The other was a wood path through the pines,
which was the one often taken by farmers living
east of the town, to shorten the distance to The
Corner.   In this road, Bounding Brook was crossed
by fording.

"Father told us to be sure to take the traveled
road if it was late," said David.

"Going to," asserted Jack, as he drew rein for a
moment, at the division of the roads.

But really, Jack was confused; the windings of
the road, with nothing but woods on each side, and,
of course, no distinct landmarks to direct them,
together with the gloom of the night and their
small acquaintance with the roads, puzzled the
boys not a little.   But Jack, being the older, wished
to impress his brother with a sense of his superior
wisdom, and would not admit his confusion.

Quickly deciding which road he would take, he
whipped up, exclaiming conclusively, "it's all
right!"

"Are you sure?" asked David.

"Certainly; I cannot be mistaken."

"I do n't know," said David.   "Let me jump off
and run to that light yonder; there must be a
cabin there."

"Oh, we can't stop for all that," said Jack. "I honestly believe this is the traveled road, David; can't you trust me?"

"But your honestly believing it, does n't make it *so!*" protested David.

"I have n't a doubt of it, Dave, you be still," cried Jack angrily.

"I think we ought to ask, so as to be sure," persisted David.

But Jack whipped up and poor David's words went to the winds, as gust after gust of the coming shower roared through the forest, and Jack urged the horse to all the speed which her heavy load would allow.

The self-willed lad was well pleased with his hasty decision, and the farther he went, the more and more convinced was he that it was the right way.

Presently the roaring of Bounding Brook arose above the noise of the tempest.

"We shall be over the bridge in a jiffy," cried Jack, "and then, old fellow, what will you say?"

"I'd like to feel myself safely over," muttered David, when, before the other could reply, Jack, David, horse, and meal went floundering into the raging waters of the swollen stream. It was pitch dark; the storm was on them, and they were miles from human help.

The first few moments of horrible suspense can scarcely be expressed. Jack at last found himself anchored on a log of drift-wood, the icy waters breaking over him, and the bridle still fast in his hand.

"David!" he shouted at the top of his voice, "David!"

"The Lord have mercy!" cried David, "I'm somewhere."

"In the raging waters of the swollen stream."

The meal? ah, that was making a pudding in some wild eddy of the Bounding Brook far below.

"No matter what a man believes, provided he's sincere," cried poor Jack, thoroughly drenched and humbled. "It's the biggest lie the devil ever got up."

"It *does* matter. *Being right* is the main thing. Sincerity does n't save a fellow from the tremendous consequences of being wrong. It can't get him

out of trouble. He's obliged to endure it, no matter how sincere he had been.

"Did n't I honestly believe I was on the right
road, when I was like going to perdition all the
time?"

The experience of that night completely and forever cured poor Jack of a common error which has
brought many a poor soul into the wild surges of
unbelief and irreligion.

SIX THINGS BEHIND

RUFUS," said his mother, "did you mail the
letter I gave you last evening?"

"Oh, mother, I forgot it! I meant to, but just
then I had to go and get some new shoe strings, so
it went out of my mind."

"Did n't I speak of those strings yesterday?"

"Yes; but just then father called me to ask if I
had weeded the pansy bed the night before."

"And had you?"

"No, mother, I was just writing the letter you
said must go to grandma—"

"I thought you were to write that on Saturday."

"I meant to, but I had to do some examples that
I did n't do on Friday, so I had n't time."

"Rufus," called his brother, "did n't you nail
the broken slat on the rabbit pen yesterday?"

"Oh!" Rufus sprang up in dismay. "I was just
going to, but I had n't watered the house plants,
and I went to do that, and then—"

"The rabbits are all out."

Rufus hastened to join in the hunt for the pets. In the course of his search he came upon two tennis rackets which he had "meant to" bring in the night before, and they were in bad condition.

"There now! It will cost ever so much to get these strung up. Why didn't I take them in, anyway? I remember I hadn't locked the stable door when father called me, and then I hurried to do it before he asked me again."

Later in the day, Rufus, with a penitent face, brought to his mother the letter which should have been mailed. During the rabbit hunt it had slipped out of his pocket, and one of his brothers had found it in the damp clover. It was now a sorry-looking missive.

THE OLD BROWN HAND

The hand that pressed my fevered brow
    Was withered, wasted, brown, and old;
Its work was almost over now,
    As swollen veins and wrinkles told.
No longer brushing back my hair,
    It gently rested on my wrist;
Its touch seemed sacred as a prayer
    By the sweet breath of angels kissed.

I knew 'twas thin, and brown, and old,
    With many a deep and honored seam,
Wearing one little band of gold,—
    The only trace of youth's bright dream:

And yet o'er every mark of care,
    In every wrinkle's mystic line,
I fancied jewels gleaming there
    That wore a beauty all divine!

Another hand my fingers pressed—
    'Twas like the lily dipped in snow;
Yet still it gave a wild unrest—
    A weariness that none should know.
There pearls with costly diamonds gleamed,
    And opals showed their changing glow,
As moonlight on the ice has beamed,
    Or trembled on the stainless snow.

I caught again the old, brown hand,
    And smoothed it fondly in my own,—
A woman's, though so old and tanned—
    A woman's—brave and fearless grown.
Aye! it had labored long and well
    To dry the tear, to soothe the pain;
Its own strong nerve to all would tell
    That life has work which brings no shame.

We love the pretty hand that rests
    In gentle fondness on our own,
With nails like rosy calyx pressed
    Upon a pearly, stainless cone;
But sacred is the healthful palm
    Which smooths the ills that round us band;
The many feel its sacred balm,
    And holy seems the old brown hand!